The return of the mysterious (a
starts a bizarre series of events
peace-loving Pat Riordan actually shooting somebody. Why did
white-hair come back? To kill somebody? To break the kneecaps
of an innocent bystander? To get some of the Monterey Bay's
wonderful seafood? Don't miss this thrilling chapter in the
somewhat exciting lives of Riordan and his peripatetic partner,
Reiko Masuda

CAROLYN KAWASHIMA
156 1/2 Tioga Avenue
San Francisco CA 94134

Happiness
Is Often
Deadly

Other books by this author:

Chinese Restaurants Never Serve Breakfast
Live Oaks Also Die
Poets Never Kill

Roy Gilligan

Happiness Is Often Deadly

Brendan Books
San Jose, CA

Art direction by Robin Gilligan
Cover art by Reed Farrington
Photography by SplashStudios
Book design and typography by Jim Cook/Santa Barbara

Copyright © 1992 by Roy Gilligan
Published by
  Brendan Books
  Post Office Box 700097
  San Jose, California 95170-0097
Manufactured in the United States of America.

1—92

Library of Congress Catalog Card Number: 91-93119
ISBN 0-9626136-3-0

This small adventure is dedicated to the memory of a man who gave us some of the most wonderfully gentle, humorous and durable radio and television shows of the past forty years,

HARRY ACKERMAN

developer of "Gunsmoke," supervisor of "I Love Lucy," developer and producer of "Bachelor Father," "Leave It to Beaver," "The Farmer's Daughter," "Bewitched," "The Flying Nun," "Gidget," and many others.

Harry did what few people seem to be able to accomplish these days. He produced shows about nice people, who seemed to be able to get along without a lot of emotional hangups. Most Hollywood people nowadays would call 'em fairy tales. But what's wrong with having the nice people win once in a while? Harry was a truly nice guy.

Once again, I must tell you that this is a piece of fiction and you shouldn't take anything seriously. I think Mark Twain said something like that once, maybe about "Huckleberry Finn."

Another nod to my favorite artist, Reed Farrington, who, in his cover portrait, captured the evil glint in the eye of the white-haired man.

My blessings on Cheryl Masuda Yemoto for *being* Reiko; my only (favorite) child, Robin, for handling the art stuff; and Jane, spouse of these many years, for keeping me honest. And my everlasting thanks to Will Smith—gentleman, scholar, and retired journalist—who edited the manuscript.

Happiness Is Often Deadly

A Short but Significant Preface

FOR A WHILE IT SEEMED to me that the white-haired man was the happiest guy in the world.

But somebody—some Greek, probably—once said that you have to be sort of stupid to be happy. Or words to that effect. Maybe he said "naïve" rather than stupid. Or maybe there's no word for "naïve" in Greek, I sure as hell don't know.

But the white-haired man seemed to have everything going for him. He got along with a cheap wardrobe. He had women pursuing him. He had to be bullet-proof because so many people would have been overjoyed to see him dead.

I thought I was reasonably happy. After a few years in Monterey, things were, well, pretty good. Oh, I have a few aches and pains. Indigestion, mostly. And what my mother used to call "aggravation in the joints." Sally Morse, who can be cruel, says it's just my age.

Reiko appeared to be happy, too. We got along pretty well, as long as I minded my own business, and didn't ask too many dumb questions. I'm not admitting that I sometimes *do* ask dumb quesions.

The firm of Riordan and Masuda, Private Investigations, wasn't making a hell of a lot of money, but who needs it? I'm kidding.

Sally seemed to be happy. That is, as long as I didn't insist on marriage. She's allergic to marriage, she says. But she's not allergic to my mysterious charms, by God. I'm not sure why she loves me, but I'm not going to ask.

It was the best of times, it was the worst of times, as another fellow said.

All of us were pretty damn' happy.

Until the (happy) white-haired man showed up in Monterey.

It was then that I learned something very disturbing. I learned that eternal bliss is probably unattainable. And, although the white-haired man was not primarily responsible for all the troubles that followed him, his reappearance began a series of nasty events that shook us all up.

I learned that happiness is often deadly.

1

"What do you suppose brought him back to Monterey?"

I SAW HIM ONE morning in October, walking down Alvarado Street, bouncing on the balls of his feet like a ballet dancer. He was dressed almost exactly as I had seen him last: black turtle neck, tight black pants, black running shoes. God, I thought he was dead, long ago.

Eric Farnham. I remembered his name. He had been butler, chauffeur and bodyguard for Felicia Montalvo, a lady of past acquaintance with a face like Dame Judith Anderson. Felicia had been a sort of queen of the rackets in Northern California until she was struck sharply by a hit-and-run driver and had her brains dashed out on the rocks off Carmel Point. Farnham disappeared shortly after the lady's demise, and I was sure that someone out of his rather checkered career in the rackets had offed him.

He was at one time, to use an old-fashioned term, an "enforcer." That is, Farnham worked free-lance for a number of casinos in the Vegas area, collecting overdue gambling debts. He would call upon a negligent client anywhere in the West, insist that he pay up, and, if money were not immediately forthcoming, break the poor bastard's knee-caps. Unfortunately, he got greedy and started skimming some of his collections. When the boys in the casinos found out, they sent a few forceful persuaders out to do unto Farnham what he had done on a number of occasions to somebody else.

That's when Felicia took him in. She had a tremendous amount of clout in Northern California. For whatever reason, she offered Farnham her protection as long as he would remain loyal to her. He did, until her death.

That was about three years ago. I guess that Tony Balestreri of the Monterey County Sheriff's Department and I were the last people on the Peninsula to see him. We had confronted him in Felicia's house, and he had more or less confessed involvement in a number of things, including the death of Sheila Lord. But that's another story.

I still picture him, in the dead of night, loping down Fifteenth Avenue to Dolores and around behind the Mission to Rio Road and thence to Highway One. What he did at that point defies my imagination. I can't see him hitch-hiking to San Luis Obispo. Not along the Big Sur Coast, man. Not in the middle of the night.

But there he was, walking down Alvarado Street. What brought him back to Monterey?

"What do you suppose brought *him* back to Monterey?"

I jumped. Reiko had been behind me, looking over my shoulder. I turned when she spoke and gave her an annoyed glare. She looked innocent, a little Asian angel, eyes as wide as their epicanthic folds would allow.

"Don't sneak up on me like that. In answer to your question, there isn't any answer. There is no earthly reason why Felicia Montalvo's white-haired boy should show himself in this town again. As a matter of fact, I was convinced that what was left of him was anchored to the bottom of some convenient body of water by a large chunk of cement. Unless. . . ."

"Unless what?"

"Unless there's something he left behind in his haste to depart. It is highly unlikely that he's still alive . . . but there he is. This is the worst possible place for him to come if he has any sense at all. He must think that everybody has forgotten him. Not a lot of respect for Tony and me. And why does he wear that goddam black outfit?"

"Buried treasure, maybe? Something of Felicia's that nobody knew about but Farnham? Or did he just get a craving for Monterey Bay seafood. There, he just went into Rosine's."

The white-haired man had indeed disappeared into one of the restaurants across the street.

"He's just hungry. That's really not a seafood house. No, babe, Farnham is back in town to get something . . . or somebody. Maybe he's back in his old profession: injuring people who can't pay their debts."

"Speaking of debts, the phone bill is on my desk . . . and the rent is due Tuesday. Are we doing anything for money?"

She had me there. Business gets pretty slow in the fall for some reason.

"We've got money coming in from a security check I did for one of those electronic widget companies. I think. Or did we spend that?"

Reiko and I are the sole employees of a sort of partnership called "Riordan and Masuda, Investigations." At least that's what it says on the window. I do most of the investigating while she cracks the whip. We have been moderately successful in Monterey, having moved the operation from San Francisco, where there are too many private investigators, lawyers and psychiatrists. What keeps us going is my connection with an obscenely wealthy man I call George Spelvin (not his right name), who has sent a lot of business my way from the snootiest levels of society on the Peninsula. Beats the hell out of snooping in back alleys. Besides, a guy could get killed that way.

My partner looked at me in much the same manner as she would contemplate some sort of pest crawling up the wall.

"Riordan, the company is very nearly broke. And I'm not going to put another nickel of Grandpa's money into it. We've just got to stir up some business."

With that, she flounced out of my office, which consists of one desk, one plastic-upholstered swivel chair I can lean back and nap in, and one uncomfortable chair for the occasional client.

I sat in my sleep-inducing swivel chair and breathed a sigh. It certainly wasn't my custom to go around knocking on doors, soliciting business. I have an ad in the phone book. George could be depended on to put me into a pending Pebble Beach divorce. But seeing the white-haired man on Alvarado Street had me hypnotized. And it wasn't very long before his presence caused me a hell of a lot of pain and suffering.

2

"I'm sure you'll remember me."

N EXT DAY, both of us had forgotten about the white-haired man. Or maybe we had both just pushed him to the rearmost position of our mental files, hoping he might go away, or that we had made an error in identification. But when I picked up the office copy of The Herald, a headline near the bottom of the front page caught my eye and gave me a bit of a start.

"Break-in at Carmel Point" it read. There weren't a lot of details. "Investigators from the sheriff's office were notified yesterday afternoon by a gardener employed by Harrison Rutledge, the home's owner, that there was evidence of a break-in. The front door of the house was ajar, and there was a light left burning in an upstairs room. Knowing that the Rutledge family was absent visiting relatives in Southern California, the gardener, Larry Sukumoto, called the sheriff. Deputies questioned on the scene said there was no doubt that someone had entered the house, but nothing seemed to be missing. (Continued on back of section, column three)."

On the back page there was a two-column picture of the house. I felt a little chill as I looked at it. I hadn't been in the neighborhood for a matter of years, but I recognized Felicia Montalvo's old lair, home of one of the greatest collections of painstakingly copied art to be found in the Western Hemisphere.

And Farnham was back in town.

I rejected a spooky feeling that Felicia had somehow risen from the dead. I had seen the old woman's body on the morning that she died, lying on the rocks with the back of her head smashed in. Reiko was probably right. Farnham had come back to get something of value he had left behind—or he knew that Felicia had left behind.

But it didn't seem characteristic of Farnham to do such a sloppy job; leaving the door open and the light on was so unprofessional. I hesitated a moment before I called Balestreri.

"Reiko, get Tony Balestreri on the phone."

"Get him yourself. You're not doing anything."

Wonderful girl, Reiko. I keep forgetting that she's my partner, and not my gofer or secretary. Sweet-tempered, agreeable child.

I swept The Herald into a crumpled mess onto the floor, and found the telephone. The number of the sheriff's office is one of four or five I have committed to memory.

Balestreri was, as usual, surly and grumbling. "Riordan, I have enough on my mind. And you're probably going to ask me for just a little bitty favor, which I will be obliged to do for you because you will remind me that I owe you one for some service of yours I cannot remember. What is it?"

"Do you remember Eric Farnham, the guy with the white hair? Felicia Montalvo's soldier? Well, I saw him in town yesterday."

He whistled. "Holy shit, I thought he was dead. Well, it just goes to show you that you can't rely on your instincts. Thanks, pal. I don't know what I'm going to do with the information, but thanks anyhow. Nice talkin' to you." And he started to hang up.

"Hold it. Obviously you don't know what is going on in your own department. Haven't you heard of the break-in on the Point yesterday? It sure as hell was in the paper. You do read the paper, don't you?"

"Only the sports and the comics, baby. So . . . a break-in on the Point. So what?"

"Felicia Montalvo's house, Tony. You remember Felicia's house. Get the connection?"

"Coincidence. The house was sold long ago. To some people from Glendale."

"Listen carefully. Yesterday, Eric Farnham appears in Monterey. Yesterday, a gardener discovers that Felicia's house was broken into.

Everybody thought Farnham was dead. Where's he been for the past three years, and why did he come back? He's still instantly recognizable. Didn't grow a beard or even bother to dye his hair."

"It isn't Felicia's house. It belongs to a family named. . . ."

"Rutledge. I know. But that doesn't mean a damn thing. Reiko and I agree that Farnham might well know that something—dope, jewels, doubloons, whatever—was hidden there. And he probably waltzed in and got it. Then he took an evening flight to San Francisco with connections for Chicago, New York, or Tokyo, and is now several thousands of miles away. So *don't* believe me."

"Our people have been all through the house. Don't you realize that *we* know that it was Felicia's house? Do you think that we are so goddam dumb we didn't go over the house with a fine tooth comb? *Nothing* was missing. Our boys checked every nook and cranny." Balestreri is a slave of the cliche, and uses every one lovingly.

"No secret panels? No fake walls? No hidden basement?" I was, you might say, disappointed.

"Zilch. Looks like somebody in the family left the door open and the light on. No bloodstains, no jimmy marks, no tell-tale footprints. Forget it, Pat."

We said the perfunctory good-byes. I felt let down. Maybe we just imagined seeing the white-haired man on Alvarado Street. But could Reiko and I have been imagining together? We're close, but not that close. Or is white hair and black clothing the latest fad of the in-crowd? I sighed as I hung up the phone. I swung my chair around and looked out the window.

A voice from behind: "Mr. Riordan? I'm sure you'll remember me. I have need for your services."

I turned very slowly. I knew the voice, the slight British inflection, the well-modulated tones.

Standing in my office doorway, leaning against the frame, distinctive in his black turtleneck, slacks and Reeboks, was Eric Farnham.

3

"She should have trusted me, you know."

I CANNOT SAY that I was struck dumb. The years have taught me not to be terribly surprised by even the most unexpected event. But I *did* have a little problem getting the following words out of my mouth: "Uh, Eric. Hi. You know the sheriff is going to be looking for you . . . for some pretty obvious reasons, uh. You *were* responsible for doping up Sheila Lord. The law thinks you are some kind of accessory to her murder, you know. Uh, what can I do for you?"

All during this little speech, I was trying to decide whether to stand up or remain seated. I would rise so that my butt was maybe six-eight inches off the chair, then sink back. Did it three or four times. Couldn't make up my mind to offer to shake hands with the man or grab him by his turtleneck and run him out of the office. I decided he looked pretty wiry, so I sank back into my protective chair and smiled weakly. All this in about fifteen seconds.

Farnham moved silently to my hard, uncomfortable client's chair and sat down. Damn thing didn't even creak. It *always* creaks when any normal human being sits on it. The man was grinning broadly. He sat very straight in the chair and grinned, his turquoise blue eyes making me very uncomfortable. After a long stage wait, he spoke:

"As a private investigator, you are obligated to keep confidential the

9

name of any client during an ongoing investigation. I am hiring you as of this moment and there's very little you can do about it. You see, I have been investigating *you,* and I know that you need money." He popped open a small leather case that was attached to his belt, and produced a familiar piece of paper. "This is a cashier's check for $5,000. See, I place it down on your desk. Now you work for me. You cannot testify against me. There is no warrant out for my arrest in Monterey County. There is no evidence linking me with Sheila Lord's death. You, my friend, are the only witness to the ill-conceived confession which I made out of sheer despondency years ago. So, are you ready to hear my proposition?"

What could I do? I *did* need the money. And Farnham was right about everything else. I watched Reiko sidle into my office and glide into a corner. There was utter fascination on her face. "Take it," she mouthed silently. "*Take* it." Farnham noticed that I was looking in another direction, and turned his head just in time to see Reiko scurry out of the room.

"The little lady is your partner, I understand. By all means, ask her to come in. I must have no secrets from partners."

She didn't need to be invited. She entered with eyes cast down, like some dutiful Japanese wife of another age, and perched on a corner of my desk. Farnham gave her legs a frankly appreciative look, but then turned to me with a face that was all business.

"No doubt you know that Felicia died intestate, and that very little of value could be found in her name. No bank accounts, no stock certificates, no nothing. That did not surprise me. The only thing that she appeared to own was that house, and when it was sold, the money was claimed by her only living relative, Sheila Lord's mother, Felicia's sister in San Jose.

"However, both you and I know that Felicia Montalvo was very, very wealthy. But what she did with her money I have no idea." He pouted for a moment. "You'd have thought she would have told *me.* But she told nobody. Not one single, solitary soul. She didn't *trust* anybody. Not even me."

The blue eyes in the deeply tanned face took on a melancholy look, and the man's lower lip protruded like a scolded two-year old's.

"She should have trusted me, you know. I would have kept her confidence. But she conducted her business conferences behind closed doors. I was always to remain in the hall, as a sort of guard. Her dining room, where she entertained her colleagues—or should I say *employees*—was virtually soundproof. Even when I glued my ear to the door, I couldn't hear a thing. . . ."

The man looked embarrassed. He had just admitted eavesdropping on his employer, and, of course, there is a certain kind of honor among thieves.

Farnham sat back and breathed deeply. "Do you understand what I want you to do, now, Mr. Riordan? Do you get my drift?"

"You want me to search for buried treasure, right? Felicia had a lot of money and it went somewhere. So far, nobody's found it. You know, of course, that the house was entered yesterday, or maybe the night before, and a light was left on. That was you, huh?"

"I still have a key. No need to force my entry. Perfectly legitimate. I did not take so much as a shrimp fork."

"Eric . . . buddy . . . you know this is an impossible undertaking. Felicia almost never went out of the house. And you were with her all the time. Except for those business conferences you were talking about. There's no answer to the question."

"That's just it, Riordan. I was *not* with her all the time. I was her errand boy. I did all the marketing. Often she sent me on other missions. I would be gone for an hour or two or more on frequent occasions. She must have seized those opportunities to do whatever she did with her income. If we were back in Worcestershire, I might have guessed that she hid her money in the basement, but most California houses don't have basements, you see. Felicia's house doesn't have one."

Farnham was reminding me that he, as an Englishman, was at least my social equal, despite his shady background.

I was thinking about the $5,000. It would go a long way for Reiko and me. I could maybe get some tires for my abused Mercedes two-seater. She could put a few bucks back into her substantial bank account. Reiko's sainted grandfather had sold his strawberry acreage to an expanding computer company in Cupertino, and left all the grandkids a goodly chunk of cash. Assuming an expression that was supposed to suggest serious consideration, I said, "Have you examined the rest of the property? Maybe the old lady buried her loot under a tree. Maybe she carted it down to the shore and secreted it in a cave among the rocks. Did you think about that?" As far as I know, there are no caves among the rocks at Carmel Point, but I had to look helpful. I was thinking of *Treasure Island* by R.L. Stevenson, who is revered on the Monterey Peninsula for having spent a couple of months here. I could see the sharp-faced Felicia depositing gold and jewels in an iron-bound chest in a cave illuminated only by fat candles. However, Farnham shook me out of the reverie.

"There's very little 'rest of the property', Riordan. A brick patio in the back to the end of the lot, and a strip of grass in front and on one side. I have examined every brick and every blade of grass. You're not much help."

Reiko, who had been uncharacteristically silent during all this conversation, finally spoke up: "What do you know about the Rutledges?"

"Who?" asked Farnham.

"The people from Glendale who bought the property. Did they buy it from the estate, or was there another owner in between."

Farnham looked surprised. "I have no idea. I *knew* the property had been sold, but the buyer's identity didn't seem to matter. Nobody else could have known about Felicia's finances. At least, I *think* I was the only one who knew. But. . . ."

He stopped speaking, but his mouth remained open and his eyes grew large. The white-haired man with the turquoise blue eyes, the black turtleneck, and the belt pouch which might have contained several other cashier's checks for $5,000, seemed to have suddenly lost his self-assuredness. His face twisted. Later, I had occasion to think that the guy could have won an Oscar for his performance that day. "How could anyone have known? Certainly not people from . . . *Glendale.*" He spat out the name of the city with unconcealed repugnance.

"I sure as hell think we'd better find out," said Reiko.

4
"He bought. Sight unseen."

I PROMISED FARNHAM that we would make every effort to find out about the present owners of Felicia Montalvo's house, bade him farewell, adjured him to keep in touch, and sent Reiko to the bank with his check. The man wouldn't tell me where he was staying. But there are so many places of lodging on the Peninsula that he might easily be in a different motel every night. He might even be at Asilomar, a state-owned conference ground which is relatively cheap and includes meals. That would be just like a cheeky Brit; hiding in a very public place, with drawers full of black turtlenecks and tight black pants.

Reiko was hot to go to Glendale to find out all she could about the Rutledge family. I had not been in the L.A. area for years, and wasn't sure just how to get to Glendale. Los Angeles is an enormous puzzle to me. When I'm there, I never know where I am. Nor am I sure how I got where I am. So I try to avoid going.

When she got back from the bank, which is on Abrego, just a couple of blocks away, I told her: "Honey, you may not need to go to Glendale. It might be just a wild goose chase. The Rutledge family is bound to return in a few days. I'm sure they know about the suspected break-in by now. Just the knowledge that their door was standing open would shake anybody up. Especially folks living in a big house on the Point, full of expensive bric-a-brac."

She looked disappointed. "OK. But if they don't show in a couple of days, I'm going. I've got a bunch of cousins in Pasadena that I haven't seen for years."

Frowning in what I hoped she recognized as deep thought, I contemplated the Rutledges. I have always been curious about families that can afford the obscene prices of some of the larger homes on the Monterey Peninsula. It's hard to believe that all those people are able to plunk down cash for a million-dollar house. And it's equally hard for *me* to imagine earning enough bucks to qualify for the kind of loan it would take to swing a deal, even with twenty or thirty per cent down. I have concluded, maybe wrongly, that the people who can buy these places are doing it with inherited money, lottery winnings, or some kind of ill-gotten gains. At least, that's what I like to think. I can't even afford to buy the little one-bedroom cottage I live in. George Spelvin (who lets me have the place rent-free) has offered to sell it to me.

"Pat," he says, "I'd like you to have the house. But I can't let it go for less than $400K, you understand. I'll finance it, if you want me to." No thanks, George. I'll just stay on. Rent-free.

There were a lot of questions to be answered. Who are the Rutledges? Why did they come to Carmel? How were they able to afford that big goddam house? Finally, did they have any prior connection, however remote, with Felicia Montalvo?

I wasn't going to get any answers just sitting on my butt in the office. I called George Spelvin.

"Rutledge? Yeah, I heard of him. Applied for membership at Cypress. You know how things are there, though. Somebody's gotta die. He's not likely to be accepted, anyhow. Committee's pretty picky. Haven't met the guy, myself. Must have a lot of dough."

"Any idea what he does for a living?"

"Not a clue. As I say, I haven't met the guy. I maybe could put you in touch with someone who has. Ed Foglia. Know him?"

"Never had the pleasure. How do I get in touch?"

"Ed's in real estate. He's got an office over on Munras. Pretty near your place, I'd think. Give him a call." George gave me Foglia's phone number. "I'd tell you to just drop in, but Ed plays a lot of golf and he's likely to be out chasin' the pill someplace."

I thanked George and hung up. When I called Foglia's office, his receptionist put me right through.

"Riordan, eh? Yeah, George has told me about you. You helped him get rid of some of his wives. Well, maybe you can help *me* some day. I haven't had as many as George, but I'm tryin'. What can I do for you?"

"What can you tell me about Harrison Rutledge? I understand you know him pretty well."

"Nobody knows Rutledge 'pretty well'. I know him as well as anybody else who's met him. He comes from down south someplace, is loaded, has a wife and a couple of kids in college, I think. I handled the sale of the house he lives in. It belonged to some old broad who didn't leave a will. When it passed to her sister, she was more than anxious to sell. The taxes would have killed her."

"Then you sold the house to Rutledge?"

"Hell, no. He *bought* it. Sight unseen. Called my office one day, and bought it for the asking price. Just like that. He called from the L.A. area somewhere and bought the house."

"You met him, though. Face to face. You talked to him. What kind of a guy does he seem to be?"

"Sorta wimpy. Smallish—maybe five-eight or -nine—about a hundred and fifty pounds. Glasses. Very soft-spoken. Limp handshake. I didn't ask him where he got the money. I don't even know if he's in business, or a dentist, or a lawyer, or what. I haven't seen him since close of escrow. Aw, wait a minute. I *did* see him. Out at Cypress. When he applied to get in. That's it."

"Ever meet his wife? His kids?"

"Wife, yes. Kids, no. Wife's a real looker. Tall blonde, taller than Rutledge. She came into the office with him one time. Didn't say a word. Just signed the papers."

I thanked the man. What he had told me wasn't much to go on. Harrison Rutledge was something of an enigma. He had been living in the Montalvo house for the better part of two years, and nobody knew him. Nobody even knew what he did for a living.

Maybe Reiko was going to be able to visit her cousins after all.

15

5

"This is Angel Garcia, Pat."

Ok, KID. You have my permission to hit the road. Why don't you call one of your thousands of cousins and arrange to stay in Pasadena. I have consulted the map, and Pasadena looks like it's right next to Glendale. But having been lost in L.A. on a number of occasions, I will guarantee nothing."

She was pleased. She has a smile that will melt tempered steel when she wants to use it. And she knows just when to use it.

"If you will make out an expense check, something in the neighborhood of a thousand dollars, I will be out of here within the hour," she said, turning the smile up to it's highest intensity.

"A thousand bucks! Now look, all I want you to do is fly down to L.A. and find out what you can about the Rutledges of Glendale. What do you need a thousand bucks for?"

"Burbank's closer, Riordan. I'll fly into Burbank, rent a car—nothing fancy, you know, just a little sub-compact—run over and stay with my cousin Charlotte, who works at Universal City, and from her place it's just a hop and a skip to Glendale, and I'll. . . ."

"Stop. I will give you the thousand. But you better bring a lot of it back."

"We'll see. I'm *presuming* on my cousin. So I have to take her and her husband to dinner. Then you've got to consider plane fare, and car rental and miscellaneous."

"What the hell kind of miscellaneous?"

"Well, *you know,* miscellaneous stuff. Like little bribes, and things like that, to get the information we need."

"We do not bribe anybody, Reiko. There are lots of legitimate channels through which we can get information."

She was way ahead of me by this time, so I was wasting my breath. She was still smiling, but she wasn't listening. I decided the best strategy was just to write the check and shut up. I did.

Reiko is very bright and very thorough. I felt sure that she would come back with all the necessary information, and about half the money. So I sent her off to the bank with the check. She went smiling out the door.

In a few minutes, she was back and on the phone with Cousin Charlotte. So many of her cousins have entirely inappropriate names; Reiko is the traditionalist who uses her Japanese name, even though most people mispronounce it. A Japanese friend of mine told me the nearest he can come to translating "Reiko" is "spectacular girl-child." Can't argue with that.

"Gotta go, Riordan. Just have time to pack a few things and catch my plane." She planted a wet kiss on my cheek and flew out the door.

She hadn't been gone five minutes when the phone made one of its bird-sounds. I picked it up and said, "Yeah?"

"Pat, this is Tony Balestreri. I think I've got something that will interest you. There's a guy in my office from Los Angeles. He's looking for information on the whereabouts of a certain Eric Farnham. Know anything about that?"

"Is the guy a cop?"

"No. He's just a guy with some business to settle with Farnham. Some pretty sticky business."

"I'll be right over."

I drove over to the sheriff's substation on Aguajito Road. Balestreri was sitting in his office talking to a very large man with very black hair and a fierce mustache. He introduced the man, reading his name from his business card. "This is Angel Garcia, Pat. Angel, meet Pat Riordan."

"That's Ahn-*hell,* Tony."

The big man grinned. "Thank you, Mr. Riordan. Most people do exactly what Sergeant Balestreri did with my name. It gets pretty painful sometimes. It's almost as bad as being Jesus." He pronounced it very carefully as "Hay-soos."

"So, what is your interest in Farnham, Angel? We know him pretty well up here."

"Mr. Riordan, I am in your business in East Los Angeles. That is, I am a private investigator. A *bilingual* private investigator." He was very proud of that "bilingual."

"Good to meet a colleague any time, Angel. What about Farnham?"

"My client is a lady—a beautiful lady—who has hired me to find Mr. Farnham. It seems that she had a strong romantic attachment for him, but he disappeared. She is a married lady, you see, and she did not want her husband to know of her, uh, attachment. So she sought me out in East L.A. She was afraid to approach an investigator in Glendale."

"Glendale?"

"Yes. Does that have any special significance?"

"Well, now, it might. What have you found so far?"

"I have managed to track Farnham to the Monterey Peninsula. And Sergeant Balestreri tells me that you saw Farnham on the street yesterday?"

"Yeah, he was going into a restaurant. Lost track of him after that." I lied cheerfully. Nothing was going to take that five grand away from me. "Angel, where are you staying? Give me your local number and I'll keep in touch. By the way, do you have any idea what Farnham was doing to support himself in Los Angeles?"

"I was never able to confirm it, but I was told by one person with whom he had come in contact that he was waiting tables in a restaurant on Cahuenga Boulevard. I'm not sure where my client met him, but they had been seeing each other for about eighteen months."

One does not sling $5,000 cashier's checks about if one works for a restaurant, even the poshest in L.A. Señor Garcia's information was going to make it necessary for me to have a good long talk with Eric Farnham.

6

I was beginning to get a bit truculent.

KNOWING THAT Farnham was somewhere on the Peninsula and finding him were two different things. I had no telephone number, and the careful white-haired man had taken pains not to tell me where he was staying. Therefore, it was somewhat serendipitous that he called me that afternoon.

It was late, and I was just about to close up shop and go home. Actually, I had been sitting in my office in a semi-trance, waiting to hear from some mysterious potential client who would propose to pay me thousands of dollars for a minimum amount of investigating. The phone rang just as I put the key in the door.

In my haste to answer it, I tripped on a waste basket and sprawled over Reiko's desk, scattering papers in all directions. I was gasping a little when I finally picked up the phone in the middle of the second bleat.

"Riordan here," I wheezed.

The bland English voice was quietly polite in my ear: "I *am* sorry, Riordan. Did I interrupt something? A bit of ear nibbling with your charming Asian friend? Or were you just dashing up the stairs for a splash of aerobics? I noticed that you do seem to be a little thicker in the middle than I remember."

"Farnham. There's a guy in town who's looking for you. A P.I. from Los Angeles. He says you ran out on a lady friend who is real anxious to see you again."

"Ah, the ladies. That has always been my downfall, Riordan. My weakness for the ladies. Did he mention this one's name?"

"You mean there might be more than one woman pursuing you? You have my sympathy and my admiration, friend. I have enough trouble with one girl at a time."

He made some sort of musing noise. "Let's see. The little redhead from Encino is out. She was altogether too demanding. I cut her off several months ago. The bikini girl from Santa Monica was a visual treasure, but quite frigid, you know. I really can't think. . . ."

"This one lived in Glendale, Farnham. Does that ring any bells?"

There was a pregnant silence. After a calculated moment, he spoke again: "The lovely Stephanie. Yes, she *would* be the one. Try as I might, I couldn't discourage her. She was ready to divorce her husband for me. Unlike the others, who would settle for dinner at a pretentious restaurant and a bottle of inferior champagne, Stephanie was desperately attached to me after I bedded her for the first time. Poor thing, she wept bitterly when I told her it was over."

"Well, she didn't forgive and forget. She hired this big Hispanic detective to track you down. And from the looks of him, he is quite able to manhandle you back to L.A."

"Oh, I doubt that, Riordan. I am descended from nobility, my friend. I am very strong. I am *pure* of heart. And very agile."

"Be that as it may. There is something that I cannot quite understand. This P.I. from L.A. says that the only means of support he could find for you down there is a job waiting tables in a fancy eating place on Cahuenga, near Universal City. I'm a little curious about that $5,000 cashier's check you handed me. Tips must be pretty good at the better Los Angeles restaurants, right?"

"Riordan, if you think I am going to reveal to you the major source of my income, you are dead wrong. Let me just say that waiting tables in a decent restaurant allows one to meet very interesting people. I will illuminate no further."

I was beginning to become a bit truculent. "You hired me to help you find what amounts to buried treasure. There is not a helluva lot to go on. I hoped you would be all up front with me. But I have a notion that you're not telling me all you know. And I can't understand why."

"I called you to find out if you're making any progress, not to answer a lot of irrelevant questions. *Have* you made any progress?"

I had to back down. "I sent Reiko to Glendale to find out what she can about the Rutledge family. Nobody around here can tell me anything about them, not even what *their* source of income is. She ought to be back day after tomorrow, at the latest. Then maybe we'll know a little more. The real estate guy who handled the sale of Felicia's house told me that Rutledge bought it by telephone, sight unseen. People just don't do that these days. Not Carmel property. Not at these prices. That's got to be the only lead I have at the moment."

"I will keep in touch. Don't call me, I'll call you. You wouldn't know where to call me anyhow, would you? And you don't know where to find me, either. But that's the way it's got to be. Ciao, Riordan." He hung up abruptly.

I sat for a while in Reiko's damnable Norwegian knee-chair, wondering whether all the hassle was worth $5,000. I had been so anxious to take the money that I hadn't really reached an agreement with Farnham. How far could I go for that amount of money? What about expenses? "Shit!" I said, out loud, and noticed that my knees were aching from the awful chair. *Was* it the Norwegians who designed it? Or the Danes? How can Reiko stand it? How can she stand to sit on her heels on that tatami mat that rests on the floor alongside her desk? It is the heritage of one whose ancestors came from across the other ocean. My own background has some roots in the rocky Aran islands off the western coast of Ireland. But I still have tender knees.

I made my way gingerly down the stairs to Alvarado Street. It was pretty dark then, and I had forgotten where I had parked my car. On gimpy legs I walked up and down the block looking for the Mercedes when it dawned on me that I had stashed it in a municipal garage up on Calle Principal.

In what was an automatic gesture for me, I swept the parking ticket out from under the wiper and crammed it into the glove compartment with the others. I have a running account with the Parking Authority. They keep giving me tickets and I keep ignoring them. Sooner or later, I pay off a bunch of them. The Parking Authority knows that. So they never go to the trouble and expense of bugging me. I pulled out of the garage and headed for home.

I was driving out Pacific Street on my way to Carmel, minding my own business, when something nasty happened. As clearly as I remember it, I was sitting at the stop sign at the intersection of Pacific and Soledad, trying to find a gap in the traffic, when somebody wacked me with a two by four. That's what it felt like, and that's what went through my mind in the split second that I remained conscious.

When I woke up in Community Hospital with Tony Balestreri leaning over me, I suddenly realized I had been shot.

7

Things slowly began to come into focus.

H'LO, TONY. How's the world treatin' you?" I asked, stupidly.

He frowned with an unnerving concern. "Do you know what happened to you? Do you remember seeing anything? Where did the shot come from? Do you have any recollection of stumbling out of your car into the middle of Soledad Drive? Scared the hell out of a woman who was on her way to Macy's. But she had presence of mind enough to stop and flag down the other traffic. You were bleeding like a stuck pig. Somebody called 911. Do you remember any goddam thing?"

He was tense and seemed a little desperate. The words tumbled out, and in my semi-lucid state I couldn't absorb all of them. "Whoa, pal. Slow down. Guess I caught one, huh? All that time on the line in Korea, and I caught my first bullet in Monterey. Ain't that the shits!"

I couldn't feel anything. Whatever they gave me at the hospital had just made me feel drunk. Me, who hasn't had a drink in what? Ten, twelve years. I was just pleasantly tight, the way (I remembered) you get on the first two or three drinks, before you have the next seven or eight and black out.

Things slowly began to come into focus. "Tony, *you* tell *me* what happened. All I can remember is that somebody hit me in the back with a board. But that's not what happened, is it?"

Balestreri sighed. "You were hit in the meaty part of the shoulder just above the collar bone with a small caliber, probably steel-jacketed bullet. It went right through the flesh, apparently on a downward flight and smashed into the glove compartment of your car. You are the luckiest bastard in the world. It must have been a hasty shot. Six inches to the left and a little lower and you'd have checked out for sure."

"Did it get my rear window? Tell me it didn't smash my rear window."

"Of course it smashed your rear window, turkey. How the hell do you think you could have been shot from the rear without the bullet breaking your rear window?"

I felt very sad about my little Mercedes two-seater. I had neglected it for years, I know. It needed fender work and paint. But for some reason, all I could think of was its smashed rear window, and the bullet in the glove compartment. At that moment I was much more concerned about my car than my wound.

By this time I was beginning to focus a little better. I looked up at the Sergeant, and asked: "Who the hell would try to kill *me*, Tony? And why? I'm a peace-loving citizen. I didn't think I had an enemy in the world. I don't carry a gun. And some sonofabitch puts a slug in me at Pacific and Soledad."

I must have been the picture of injured innocence. Balestreri put his hand on my arm and gave it a reassuring squeeze. "We're trying to find out. That is, the Monterey cops are trying to find out. You were out of my jurisdiction. One of the nurses remembered your being up here when I was shot, and that you're my friend. That's the only reason I'm here."

Slowly, as I was becoming fully conscious, I became aware of a deep ache in my right shoulder. I glanced down and saw that a massive bandage covered my right shoulder, and that my right arm was immobilized by wrappings that kept it in a crooked position so that my fist was just a few inches under my chin.

"How the hell am I going to eat like this? Don't they know I'm right-handed? This is ridiculous."

A nurse's head appeared over Balestreri's shoulder. "Mr. Riordan, I'm sorry, but it will be necessary to keep your arm restrained for a few days. It's really better than putting it in a cast, don't you think? We're just happy that you didn't need extensive surgery. Bullet wounds do terrible damage, you know."

Guns put holes in people. I saw a lot of people, some of 'em close friends, with holes in them from guns in Korea. Now I had a hole in *me.* I hate guns.

The investigator in me took over. "What do the police know, Tony? Are there any witnesses? Anybody see anything?"

Balestreri took out his notebook. "It happened very quickly. There were several cars lined up behind you at that intersection. I assume you were waiting to turn left over to Munras to get up to Highway One. Going home, eh?"

"Yeah, yeah, yeah. So, answer my questions."

"A guy in the third car behind you thinks he heard a shot. Or it could have been a backfire, y'know. Anyhow, you were first in line at the stop sign. The traffic coming north was pretty heavy. Directly behind you was a pickup, one of those high-rise jobs, y'know, with the big tires. When you got out of your car and collapsed in the intersection, the guy in the third car said the pickup pushed your car into the intersection—it almost ran over you—and turned right up Soledad. He was so concerned with your body in the street that he didn't pay much attention. But, as I think about it, the shooter had to have been in the truck to get the angle on you."

"Didn't anybody see the bastard shoot? He had to hang out of the cab to get a bead on me."

"Sorry, Pat. You know how those things are. Everybody is lost in his own thoughts. Nobody notices anything, or gives a damn. The guy in the truck probably could have got out and climbed in with you to shoot you, and nobody would have paid any attention. They were probably all going home from work, sweating out the traffic."

"Nobody got the license number of the truck? Nobody could tell what color it was, or what year it was? Goddam blind public!"

"I'm *sorry,* Pat. Maybe something else will turn up. I'll keep in touch with the Monterey cops. And, of course, one or two of them will be wanting to talk with you. You sure you have no idea who would try to kill you?"

"A crazy old man took a shot at me a couple of years ago when I was getting too close in an investigation. But he later shot himself. In my presence. The Red Chinese sent a lot of people to kill me, but they missed. No, there is nobody out there trying to kill me. That I know of. Unless. . . ."

"Unless what?"

"I keep thinking about that Angel Garcia from Los Angeles. Not that he would have any reason to off me. But there's something more to that business of his than just tracking down Farnham for a spurned lover. I just have a feeling."

"One, Garcia was having dinner with me when you were shot. Two, he drives an '86 Toyota Camry. Three, he. . . ."

"Never mind. I've got an almost death-bed confession to make, Tony. Eric Farnham hired me for some special snooping. But, believe me, I don't know where he is. He paid me a lot of money in advance, but he didn't tell me where he was staying, or how I can get in touch with him. That's the truth."

Balestreri didn't seem surprised or disturbed. "You shouldn't have told me that, sport. But I forgive you. We're not really looking for Farnham at the moment. *But* if we *do* start lookin' for him, you'd better be ready to cooperate."

"One more thing, Tony."

"Yeah"

"What day is it?"

8

"Pat, my God, what happened?"

It WAS THURSDAY. Just after 12 noon. I had been shot on Wednesday evening at about six-twenty by perpetrator or perpetrators unknown. A little over eighteen hours had passed. Suddenly, I was angry.

"Goddamit, Tony, there's no excuse for, uh, inconveniencing me like this. I was mucking along, minding my own business. Farnham wouldn't shoot me. I don't even know where he is. I haven't had a chance to get anywhere on the job he wants me to do. All I've done was send Reiko to Glendale to find out about Harrison Rutledge. . . ."

I blew it. Balestreri looked at me sharply. "What did you say? You sent Reiko to find out about Rutledge? What the hell has Rutledge got to do with this business?"

"Privileged information, Sergeant. Can't tell you anything about it. Loose lips sink ships and all that. Why don't you go out and catch some criminals? Can't you see I'm delirious or something?"

Balestreri shrugged. "OK, Pat, I'll go. But remember what I said. You had goddam well be ready to cooperate when and if we should need you." He stood up wearily and left the room.

For the first time I was able to examine my surroundings. I was in the conventional hospital bed. To my left was a window with a charming view of the parking lot. To my right was one of those drapes suspended from a track to afford a bit of privacy to one patient or the other in a semi-private room. I could only guess that there was somebody in the other bed. On a table between my bed and the drape was an assortment of things, including a telephone. Also on my right, hooked to the bed frame, was the signal for the nurse. I tried reaching the phone with my left hand and felt a searing pain in my right shoulder. A similar effort to reach the nurse's signal got the same result. "What the hell am I supposed to do," I said out loud, "yell for the nurse when I have to pee?"

A bored voice came from beyond the drape. "Just tell me, pal. I'll ring her bell."

I was embarrassed. "Sorry, buddy. And thanks. Ah, what are you in for?"

"Busted tibia. Got it while fleeing from my wife. Please don't ask me why."

"Friend, I am the soul of discretion. And I am extremely curious about why you were running from your wife."

The man h'mmed a long, drawn out h'mm. "H'mmm. Well I might as well. You and me are ships that pass in the night, right? Well, the wife found out about me romancin' another lady. She chased me out of the house. I fell over a fire hydrant and busted my tibia. Seems she heard all about it in the beauty parlor. From her aesthetician."

"Her what?"

"Her aesthetician."

"What's an aesthetician?"

"How the hell should I know? But she has one."

At that moment the phone on my bedside table rang. I called out desperately: "For God's sake somebody get the phone. I can't reach the bleeping thing."

My roommate swept aside the drape, hopped on one foot to my table and picked up my phone. He was a tall thin man with a scraggly beard and calloused hands. "208 B, who do you want?" He pulled the phone down and covered the receiver. "You Riordan?" I nodded. He handed me the phone and hopped back to his bed, pulling the drapes closed behind him. I never saw him again. Hope he patched up things with the wife.

"Hello," I said weakly into the phone.

"Pat, my God, what happened?" It was Sally Morse, the lady I like to spend my leisure hours with. "Tony Balestreri called me a couple of minutes ago and said you had been shot. How could that be?"

"Sally, what's an aesthetician?"

"What?"

"An aesthetician. The guy in the next bed tells me that his wife found out about his playin' around from her aesthetician. Never heard the word before."

"Neither did I. But who gives a damn. How are *you?*"

"Pretty good. Pain now and then. But they give me some stuff to cut it down. Feel a little drunk with it, Sal. And you know I haven't. . . ."

"Had a drink for ten years or more. I know. Who shot you?"

"Some guy in a pickup, I think. Although I have no idea why. You sure you never heard of an aesthetician?"

"Sounds like something somebody made up to make 'beauty operator' sound like a dignified profession. What have you been up to, Pat? I mean, why would anybody shoot you?"

"I *said* I've got no idea. But why don't you come over here this evening and bring a cake with a file in it."

Sally's voice quavered. "Dammit, Riordan, I am *deeply* concerned about you, you miserable sonofabitch. And you make dumb jokes. I *will* come to see you this evening. And I will hold your stupid hand. But don't kid with me about this."

She can always make me feel guilty, somehow. Even when I'm the injured party. I was apologetic.

"Honey, I'm gonna be all right. Just need a few days rest. Yeah, come see me . . . and hold my hand." We said goodbye, as if we were two teen-age kids who felt deep affection for one another, but were too shy to show it.

Since I had the phone and its cradle in my hands, I just rested it on my stomach until somebody could take it away.

There was some murmuring over by the door. In a moment, a small, dapper man came smiling around the drape and into my area.

"Mr. Riordan? I'm Lieutenant Baker of the Monterey Police. Do you feel well enough to answer a few questions?"

"Never better, Lieutenant. Sorry I can't offer you some coffee or something."

The smile got even wider. "Good to see you in such excellent spirits, Mr. Riordan. That must have been a painful wound."

"Yeah, it hurt some. So what have you found out about the guy who shot me?"

"Very little, I'm afraid. That's why I'm here. I thought maybe you could shed a little light on the mystery."

"As far as I know, nobody's mad at me. Mad enough to *shoot* me, that is. You probably know my business. Well, I can't tell you what I'm working on currently, but I'm sure there's no grounds for attempted assassination. There, the ball is in your court."

He sighed, still smiling. "We believe that you were shot by a person driving a pickup which had apparently been following you. The person took advantage of the long wait at the stop sign at Pacific and Soledad to make his or her move. Several witnesses saw the pickup bump your car and then pull out suddenly and move at high speed north on Soledad just after the shot. Unfortunately, nobody thought to get a license number. However, one witness described the driver. He, or she, wore dark glasses and a hard hat. That's it."

"That's zip, Lieutenant. Anybody notice a dog in the pickup? A guy with a hard hat and dark glasses driving a pickup must have had a dog. We've got thousands of guys driving pickups, wearing hard hats, but they all have dogs. Now, if we could identify the dog, we'd be somewhere."

The smile faded slightly, then returned in full bloom. "I'm sorry to have disturbed you, Mr. Riordan. If you think of anything that could help us in this matter, please call me." He laid a business card on my table, gave a soft salute, and disappeared. I closed my eyes, and went to sleep.

9

I felt anger rising in my bosom.

THE PHONE VIBRATED on my chest. I was dimly aware of the strange sensation. In my drugged state I had been dreaming very odd dreams. Somehow or other, Sally was massaging my chest and I was massaging hers. Would you call that an erotic dream? It didn't seem so in my comatose condition. Then the vibrating continued persistently until I roused sufficiently to hear the accompanying sound, and, after considering the matter for a while, tried to reach for the phone with my right hand.

The pain had me wide awake in seconds. It all came back: the wound, the hospital, the guy in the pickup truck. Reason returned and I picked up the phone with my left hand. "H'lo," I said, weakly.

It was Reiko's voice. "It's me, Riordan. Can't I leave you for a couple of days without having you get in some kind of trouble?"

"How'd you know I was here? Who told you?"

"I called the office. Four times. When I couldn't get you there, I tried your house. I figured something was wrong, so I called Tony. *He* told me."

"Are you calling from Pasadena? Long distance? What time is it? Don't you know you have to wait until after eight o'clock to get the best rate? Are you charging this to the office?" It wasn't like me to be so concerned about expenses. I had never stinted on my business trips. But there I was, reading Reiko out for running up a phone bill. I *must* have been out of my head.

"Forget it. I'm calling from Charlotte's. She piles up so much long distance she'll never notice this call on her bill. What I want to know, dammit, is how are you? Tony said you were getting along well, but then he described how you were shot, and I'm not satisfied. *You* tell me."

"Aside from being in severe pain and weakness from loss of blood, I am just fine. You woke me up. I'm just a little giddy from the medications they've been pumping into me. There's a very pretty nurse taking care of me, but I can't for the life of me think what she looks like right now. I feel very much like I have to pee, but I can't reach the signal button. And my roommate seems to have departed." I twisted my neck over to the right and confirmed the empty bed.

"I'm relieved," she said. "When I hear you talk like that, I figure you're recovering rapidly. Any idea who shot you and why?"

"It's a totally new development. Nobody has any real reason to kill me. And that's what I'm sure the miscreant was trying to do. I feel strongly that if he—or she—was just trying to scare me, he—or she—would not have put the bullet *through* me but just somewhere *around* me. Or maybe the perpetrator was just a goddam bad shot."

"Stay cool, Riordan. Nobody's going to bother you in Community Hospital. I'm coming home Saturday morning, and I'll be right straight out to see you. I have picked up some surprising information about the Rutledge family."

"For God's sake, don't keep me in suspense. What about the Rutledge family?"

"Hold it, Riordan. It's nothing I can do justice to on the phone. You'll just have to wait."

I felt anger rising in my bosom. But almost immediately, I realized that it was just a reaction to *everything.* The feeling subsided as quickly as it came.

"OK, sweetie. I will wait for your report. Meanwhile, what the hell is an aesthetician."

"What?"

"An aesthetician. E–s–th–. . . Oh, shit. Do you know what it is?"

"Never heard the word. Is it in the dictionary?"

"I haven't looked," I nearly shouted. "But don't let it bother you. Just get here. ASAP."

She said some sort of goodbye, and hung up. I replaced the phone in its cradle on my chest and wondered who was going to put it back on the table, when Sally Morse came in.

Sally came to my bedside with a positively funereal look on her face.

"How are you, darling?" she said, warmly clasping my free hand.

"I have to pee. Could you ring for the nurse?"

Taken aback, she hesitated for a moment and then reached for the nurse's signal. "Can't you think of anything else to say to me, Pat? I've *really* been worried about you."

"Honey, I have to go to the bathroom. I love you and all that, but if I am not permitted to pee in something soon, I will embarrass the both of us by wetting the bed."

The nurse arrived, and soon I was presented with a peculiar plastic device with an appropriate neck on it. I shooed Sally out of the room, and relieved myself into the bedside urinal. Feeling refreshed, I called out for Sally to come back in the room.

"Why'd you do that?" she asked.

"What?"

"Chase me out of here while you . . . *you* know."

"I feel that a man should have a little dignity when he pees in a bottle, that's why."

"Look, Riordan, I have seen you in all states of undress. Did you think I'd be shocked?"

I had no real answer for that one. I changed the subject.

"Did you ever find out what an aesthetician is?"

"Somebody told me it's a beauty operator who deals with the skin. Like hair removal, makeup, and the like."

"Aesthete. One who appreciates beauty. Begins with an 'a' not an 'e'. Ah, *hah.*"

"You are impossible. Who the hell cares that much about words? How are you feeling?"

"Wonderful, give or take an unbearable pain now and then. Thanks for asking."

Sally is a terrific girl. She's edging into her mid-forties, maybe ten or twelve years younger than I am. She's intelligent and beautiful. A tallish girl, with gray-streaked auburn hair, she runs a travel agency and makes more money than I do. So far, she has refused to marry me, even though we are devoted to each other. She had one bad bout with marriage, and I guess she's gun shy. I had a good marriage, but

Helen was killed in an autombile accident, and Sally is the only woman I've found who could come close to taking her place.

She leaned over and kissed me very tenderly. I put my good arm around her neck and pulled her to me. At that moment I could see her eyes roll up in alarm, as I heard the voice of Eric Farnham from the other side of the bed.

"I do hope I'm not interrupting anything important. Really, Riordan, it was careless of you to get shot. But of course, I'm awfully glad you're alive. I just had to come and see for myself."

The white-haired man, in his usual costume, was standing by my bed with a malevolent smile on his tanned face.

10

"How could you be associated with a man like that?"

SALLY, A LITTLE FLUSHED, stood up hastily and started to smooth out her dress. Farnham favored her with a wide and toothy smile, and waited expectantly.

"Sal, this is, uh, a client of mine. Eric Farnham. Eric, Sally Morse. I told you about Eric, didn't I, honey. We go back some years." The painkiller and the sedatives I had been given were making me a little looney.

"What an extraordinarily handsome lady, Riordan. Surely you don't deserve her." Farnham was talking to me, but looking at Sally.

Sally did not know quite how to react to Farnham. She stood tall beside my bed, all five-ten of her, and extended her hand. "Nice meeting you," she said. But she didn't mean a word of it.

"Who shot you?" said the white-haired man. "Anybody I know?"

"As a matter of fact, Eric, I thought it might be you. Not for any particular reason. But knowing about your professional activities, I just kind of felt that you'd decided to dispense with my services."

"After giving you $5,000? You're crazy, man. Are you sure that bullet didn't go through your brain? Many things, negative and otherwise, might be said about me. But never would I waste that kind of money."

"OK. Then what brings you here? Don't you know there is a large gentleman from East L.A. in town looking for you? He might even now be observing outside, waiting for you to depart."

"Riordan, you are tiresome. No, I did not shoot you. Yes, I came here to check on your condition. No, I was not followed by the man from Los Angeles. Yes, I am a *professional,* and letting somebody like that track me would be amateurish. Do you know anything yet?"

"Goddamit, how could I know anything? I've been in this bed for nearly twenty-four hours. Give me a telephone number, and I'll call you Saturday. There might be something by then." I carefully avoided telling him anything about Reiko's report from Glendale.

"Right-o, old boy. But *I'll* call *you* on Saturday. At your office? In the morning?"

"At my office. In the afternoon. I don't ordinarily go in on Saturday, but for you, I'll make an exception. That's damned decent of me, isn't it?"

Farnham smiled broadly at Sally, and touched his brow with two fingers. As abruptly as he had appeared, he vanished out the door.

Sally had this stupid look on her face. Now, Sally doesn't look stupid ordinarily. As a matter of fact, I had never before seen her look stupid. But Farnham has that effect on people.

"What was that all about? How could you be associated with a man like that? He looks like a thug. Does he always wear that black turtleneck and those tight black pants?"

"He is a thug. He was involved in a case I worked on before I met you. And, yes, he always seems to wear the same cat-burglar outfit. Please don't press me further."

"Isn't there a chair around here? I'm tired and I want to sit down. Where's a goddam chair?"

It wasn't like her to swear like that. She's a lady of considerable refinement. "I think there's one over by the other bed. But I can't get it for you, Sal. You're on your own."

She walked across the room and seized the small chair with one hand, brought it to my bedside, and sat down with a long sigh. "Have you ever thought of getting into another profession, Pat? Want to go into the travel business with me? I think we could do pretty well together."

"I have often thought of getting into another business, but I'm too old to change. After nearly thirty years in this racket, I think I know what I'm doing. I don't want the responsibility of having to learn a whole new set of tricks. Old dogs, you know."

A nurse's aide arrived with a tray of unidentifiable hospital food. I discovered that I was hungry, but nothing on my plate appeared to be edible. There was some green stuff, some yellow stuff, and a piece of meat that looked like it had been charred over an open flame. I made a stab at it with my left hand, but failed miserably. Patient Sally cut my meat, which was fuzzy and tasted like styrofoam, and spooned some of the green and yellow stuff into my mouth. She also helped me with the dessert, which I could recognize as a watery custard.

After eating, I felt terribly tired. Sally stayed with me until visiting hours were over. I can't remember what we talked about. Then she left me with a squeeze of the hand and a peck on the cheek. And I fell into a deep and dreamless sleep. A sleep from which I might not ever have awakened.

The noise that woke me at what I later learned was about three a.m. was the sound of a small caliber pistol with a silencer. A sort of metallic "splat." Instinct made me roll out of the bed, landing on my good left shoulder on the cold hospital floor. I didn't notice the stabbing pain right away. When I peeked over the bed, a figure was just going out the door. There was the smell of gunpowder in the air and a cloud of gray smoke. And there was a neat hole in the pillow of the bed next to mine.

11

"Any nitwit could have killed me."

I HAVE OFTEN thought that the Community Hospital of the Monterey Peninsula would be a good place to die. But I really wasn't ready yet, not at all. Being rudely awakened by gunshot in that charming establishment on the picturesque ridge that separates Monterey from Pebble Beach was not a tranquilizing experience.

Probably the whole wing of the hospital heard me yell. I'm not one who screams for help ordinarily. Call me Joe Cool most of the time. But that night I panicked. And in minutes there were nurses and doctors and aides and God knows who else in the room with me, looking anxiously at the man in 208 B, a gunshot case with a very loud voice.

"What happened?" said a large blonde nurse, straining to preserve her nursely calm. Everybody else just stood and gaped.

"Somebody was in here about a minute and a half ago with a gun. Somebody fired a shot with a silencer. Somebody was dumb enough to think I was in the other bed." I stopped. Why did the shooter put a slug in the other bed? There was light enough in the room to see that that bed was empty, and that I was lying on my back in the other one with my mouth open, snoring loudly. There's no rhyme or reason in this, thought I. Anybody who really wanted to kill me could have walked right up to my bed and put a fatal bullet in me from a distance of one foot. Was it the same person who shot me in the car? I thought that the man—or woman—was just a lousy shot. But now I wasn't sure.

The large blonde nurse seemed to discover, much to her amazement, the hole in the pillow on the other bed. She bent down to examine it, and all the others, including a very young doctor with baggy eyes and a stethoscope dangling from his neck, gathered around her.

"Who did this?" she demanded, as if she held me directly responsible for damaging the linen service. "Who did this, and why?" She pushed the young doctor out of the way and came to my bed. Leaning into my face close enough for me to count the pores in her nose, she asked, "Did you know the person who did this?"

"Hell, I only saw the person for a split second. His—or her—ass was three-quarters out the door when I opened my eyes. Do me a favor. Call Sergeant Balestreri of the Sheriff's Department. Tell him what happened and say Riordan sent you." I gave them Tony's number.

Slowly the group moved out the door in silence. The last in line, a nervous-looking aide picked up the pillow with the hole in it and started to carry it off.

"Whoa! Leave that where it lies. Wait till the cops get here. Then you can put a nice clean one in its place"

I wasn't going to go back to sleep that night. I mean, there are *certain* things that shake you up pretty good, and, having already been a gunshot victim, I was indeed shook up. I suppose I lay there alone, staring up at the ceiling for most of an hour before Tony Balestreri burst in.

"Holy shit, Riordan, what kind of mess are you in. First you get a bullet in you. Then somebody tries to finish the job in the hospital. Look, you've got to tell me what you're doing for Farnham. I have a notion that *he's* the guy who's trying to help you into the afterlife. Come on, baby. Start talking."

"First, I don't think anybody is trying to kill me. I think the guy in the truck hit me by accident. I *know* that the person who put that shot in the pillow did it on purpose. Any nitwit could have killed me. It took some doing to put a slug in the wrong bed. No, my friend, somebody is just trying to scare me off."

"Be that as it may, you've got to tell me what it is you're working on for Farnham. You and I know the guy is trouble. And we know what kind of trouble, don't we? Don't give me any shit about confidentiality this time, Riordan. What's Farnham's problem?"

I tried to explain the details of my deal with the white-haired man without giving too much away. I told Tony that Farnham was looking for some loot he believed was stashed somewhere on Carmel Point, and he wanted me to help him find it. I left out the fact that Reiko was in Glendale investigating the Rutledge family, and did not mention Farnham's visit to the hospital.

"So the old lady stashed her ill-gotten gains where nobody can find 'em, eh? What a downer. But what the hell do you think you can do to locate Felicia's treasure?"

I was hurt. "I can help. I know the Point. I know the Peninsula. I knew Felicia. And I have a few pretty good ideas. You wound me, Tony. You denigrate my professionalism. You. . . ."

"Stuff it. Where'd the bullet hit?"

I indicated the pillow on the other bed. Balestreri walked over to it, sniffed it, picked it up, turned it over, and began to feel it with erotic action of the fingers, trying to locate something inside.

"Bullet didn't come out the back. Gotta still be in here. Umm. Yeah. Oh, yeah. Here's the little bastard."

Carefully, he worked the slug around to the entry hole and popped it out into his palm.

"Twenty-two. Not much velocity. Just enough to penetrate but not enough to pass through. These hospital pillows are pretty dense. That's very peculiar."

"What's very peculiar?"

"The slug that I dug out of your dash was steel jacketed, with enough power behind it to penetrate your rear window, a piece of you, and smash through your glove compartment. The two bullets might have come from the same gun. Ballistics will tell us. Either there were two different shooters or whoever shot you in the car and missed you here loads his own. I'd judge he's a target shooter with a long-barreled twenty-two."

"Or *she*. Lots of women like to shoot. And you've got to remember that the female of the species is more deadly than the male. I think Kipling said that first. Or maybe it was Robert W. Service. But it's accurate."

"Go back to sleep. Tell the nurse to give you a shot of something. They got me out of a nice warm bed to come over here and now I'm awake until I drop from exhaustion at the end of my shift at midnight. Am I the only guy in the Sheriff's Office you know?"

"You're the nicest, Tony. I've always said that. I've told Reiko a hundred times that Balestreri is a real prince, even though he bitches a lot. Thanks for coming."

"Bullshit," he said, and went out the door.

12

"Did you spend all the money?"

THE NEXT DAY went by very quickly. I was still being shot full
of demerol or something similar from time to time, and I got the
notion that the medical people were concerned about the possibility of
infection in the hole in my shoulder. They still kept my right arm
trussed up against my body, although I pleaded with them to cut me
loose. From what Balestreri had told me, I knew the bullet had passed
through the big muscle that connects my shoulder and my neck. Later
I found out that it had creased my collar bone, and *that* was the reason
for the sling.

I was beginning to feel like a fallen warrior in the battle against
crime. I ate the awful hospital food in a manly fashion, and drank the
glasses of unidentifiable juice that were presented to me in mid-
morning and mid-afternoon. I called for television service, and
watched soap operas and game shows, attractions that were otherwise
anathema to me. I even got interested in something called "Loving",
and made a mental note to catch the show at home when I could. Lots
of steamy sex and good-looking women.

The only visitor I had, other than Lieutenant Baker of the Monterey
Police, was my old friend George Spelvin. Sally had told him of my
plight.

"George Spelvin" is just a name by which I refer to this very rich guy who, as I've told you, owns the house I live in, and was directly responsible for my coming to Monterey. It's a phony name, made up on Broadway to slip into a program for an anonymous actor. I have sworn never to reveal his true identity because of possible embarrassment to his aristocratic family. I've kept my word.

"My God, Riordan," he said, rushing into the room, "what did you do to get yourself shot?"

That's George, all right. Comes right to the point. Doesn't consider that I might have been an innocent victim.

"First, I don't think anybody was trying to shoot me. There's evidence that somebody was *trying* to scare hell out of me." I tried to indicate my right shoulder and winced with pain. "I've got a hole up here through the muscle, and a few inches to the left would have finished me. If the bullet had busted through the right carotid artery, I'd have checked out before I checked in here. And, George, I really am innocent. I don't think I have offended anybody."

He looked a little sheepish. "Sorry, old man. It's just that I think of you as invulnerable, the last person in the world to get shot. You're a white-collar private eye. You always steer clear of the rough stuff. But somebody shot at you. How do you explain it?"

I took a deep breath. "I took a job for a guy who has an unsavory reputation. I shouldn't have taken it, but I needed the money. It's almost as simple as that."

"So, did this guy try to kill you because you blew the job, or what?"

"No, no, George. I don't think *he* had anything to do with the shooting. But somebody who *knows* him might have done it. Please don't ask me any more."

"What about this guy Rutledge? You asked me about him. Did you get in touch with Foglia?"

"That's unfinished business. I sent Reiko to L.A. to find out about the Rutledge family. She phoned to tell me she had dug up something, but she wouldn't tell me what it was. She's due back tomorrow morning."

"Jesus, man, I was about to call you when Sally called *me*. Friend of mine just moved out on his wife. Needs help. Wants to divorce her, but can't think of a good reason. She can really take him for a ride, and he is loaded, pal. She's his fourth, he's her fifth. She took the pants off the other four guys. My friend doesn't want it to happen to him."

"He should have kept his pants on in the first place, George. That's what I can't understand about your crowd. You can't just sleep with 'em, you have to marry 'em. Tell your boy I'll be out of here in a few days, and I'll do what I can."

George sat down wearily on the little chair at my bedside. He's a handsome man in his mid-sixties, slender, tanned, with an expensive haircut and a short gray beard. He's had quite a bit of work done on his face by overpriced plastic surgeons, but when he's tired all the seams and creases show, and he looks his age. I think that he really likes me, even though he probably knows by now that I once had a one-night stand with his current wife. But he certainly didn't hear that from me. Debbie Spelvin, God bless her, is out of jail now. I had a lot to do with putting her in. George's lawyer copped a second degree plea for her in the death of Sheila Lord. But that's in the past. George has forgiven me.

"I'll have the guy get in touch," he said. He looked out the window. "I can get you a room with a better view. My family gave this place a lot of dough. Let me talk to the administrator. Jeez, all you can see is the parking lot."

"Never mind, George. I think I'll be out of here by tomorrow afternoon. At least, that's what they tell me now."

George left me with some mumbled wishes for a speedy recovery. He isn't one to get over-emotional.

As I lay in that hospital bed, I began to go over the events that occurred just prior to my being shot. Nothing made a hell of a lot of sense. The shock of seeing Farnham on Alvarado Street was the catalyst for everything. It all started with that moment. From then on it was like a bad dream. The nerve of the sonofabitch to come to me for help. The $5,000 cashier's check. The fact that Farnham wouldn't tell me where he was staying, or what phone number he could be reached at. And the whole mish-mash about the Rutledge family and who the hell they were.

It was all I could do to eat the brown stuff and the green stuff on my hospital tray that evening. I even gagged a little on the Jello. And it was very hard for me to ignore the little glass of wine they gave me.

I watched the TV that night until my eyes glazed over, the big blonde nurse came in with a hypodermic needle full of something and jabbed it into my butt, and I went to sleep.

When I opened my eyes the next morning, Reiko was there. She reached out and took my good hand.

"Did you spend all the money?" was the first thing I asked.

"Really, Riordan. Aren't you glad to see me? I'm sure happy to see you. I was thinking about you all the way here. I came up just as soon as my plane landed."

"How the hell did you get in here before visiting hours?"

"My cousin Dan Murikama is Chief of Surgery here. I just used his name. You've met Dan, haven't you?"

I should be used to the fact that Reiko has innumerable relatives spread all over California. But when another one turns up, I am always surprised.

"Hey, what about the Rutledges? You said on the phone you had some sort of dirt on them."

She smiled smugly. "I made very discreet inquiries in their neighborhood. I checked out all their known activities. Mr. Rutledge doesn't seem to do anything for a living. But he wasn't home very much of the time. Gone for weeks, the neighbors said. But one old snoopy woman who made a habit of watching the movements of all the neighborhood folks told me something that should be meaningful." She paused, dramatically. "Mrs. Rutledge had a frequent visitor when her husband was gone. He'd arrive at all times during the day or night. Their kids were away most of the time at college in the East. But this was a very interesting visitor. A man about five-ten, white hair, deep tan, always dressed in black. Sound like anybody you know?"

"Quick, what's Mrs. Rutledge's first name?"

"Stephanie," she said, as she sat back in the chair, expecting my gratitude.

"Remind me to give you a raise."

"You can't do that. I'm your partner."

"Then bend over and let me kiss you. You have illuminated my life."

13

It was certainly <u>not</u> Eric Farnham.

REPORT FROM Reiko Masuda, investigator:
I'm going to write all this stuff out, because if I don't, I'll forget
something. Please forgive the way I have done this. Formality ain't my
thing. This won't really sound like a police report, but those things are
boring, anyhow.

The trip down was pretty dull. On the plane I sat next to a lady who
was flying for the first time, and I sort of had to hold her hand. Not
really, of course. But I did pat her on the arm now and then. The flight
was routine. Some bumps over the Valley as we turned in to Burbank,
but nothing to fret over.

My cousin met me at the airport. She had taken off work for the
afternoon. She's in the office at Universal City, you know, *not* out
where the shark is or the King Kong. You'd probably come up with
some wise remark about any relative of mine being able to scare the
hell out of a crowd of tourists. So I just threw that in.

Anyhow. Charlotte drove me to her apartment in Pasadena. We
talked a lot about family and old times, and like that. Then it dawned
on me that I'd have to have a car. I called on of the car rental places
and they were pleased to deliver a little Ford Escort first thing the next
morning.

So. The next morning I drove over Colorado Bouleva
dale. Did you know that's where the Rose Parade is? You dr
the Rose Bowl. It's down in sort of a canyon, a really
location. I remember when my father used to bring us dow
Rose Parade. One of his brothers owned a store right on Colorado
Boulevard and we used to watch the parade from the second story
window. Never went to the game. Papa didn't like football at all.

But I'll bet you're wishing I'd get down to business, aren't you. Well,
the first thing I did in Glendale was check in at the library. Why didn't
I look in the phone book? you say. Well, the library has a complete set
of phone books, dummy. Besides, the book at Charlotte's place didn't
cover Glendale. Do you have any idea how many phone books there
are in Los Angeles? God, if they tried to get the whole place in one
book, it'd be two feet thick.

I found a listing for Harrison Rutledge in the phone book. Looks
like he kept his place here even after buying the house in Carmel. But,
since I was at the library, I went to the newspaper files to see what I
could see. Took me the entire morning. But I found some things about
Rutledge and his wife, some social notes. They've only been married a
few years. The kids are hers. In all the stories that have anything about
them, he's referred to as an entrepreneur, whatever that means.
There's no mention of his business or anything.

Anyway. I drove out to the address I found in the phone book. It's
beautiful, I mean expensive, next to luxurious. You'd find stuff like
this in Beverly Hills or Bel Air, but I didn't expect it in Glendale.
When I knocked on the door, nobody answered. I knocked again and
rang the bell, and nobody answered. I was just about to take off when
a pool maintenance truck pulled up. I asked the pool man about the
Rutledges. He was a kind of talkative guy, and he was perfectly willing
to give me all the gossip he knew.

It was believed, he said, around the neighborhood, that Harrison
Rutledge was connected to the rackets. That's what the folks were
saying. Before he bought the house in Carmel, he would stay in this
house for days, even weeks. The wife would go out frequently, sometimes overnight. But Rutledge never seemed to leave. A lot of folks
didn't believe that a wimpy little guy with glasses could be involved in
anything illegal. But a divorced lady across the street, who spent lots of
hours observing the comings and goings at the Rutledge house, swore
that he had to be into dope or something to afford a house like that

with no visible means of support. Lately, the woman told the pool guy, after he bought the house in Carmel, he'd be gone for a week at a time. That's when she noticed the visits of the white-haired guy in the black clothes.

When the pool guy had gone, I checked with the snoopy lady across the street. She was happy to see me. I think she would have been happy to see anybody. She invited me in for a cup of tea, and before the water got hot, she was telling me the same things that the pool man had told me. The woman really kept tab on the Rutledge family. She had made a hobby of observing them from the minute they moved in. They weren't very friendly at all, she said. Never made a move to visit her. And when she went over to their house to welcome them to the neighborhood, she was kept on the front stoop while Mrs. Rutledge smiled sweetly in the doorway, never taking her hand from the knob.

The across-the-street lady told me her name was Clarice Maxwell (Mrs.), and that her husband, the sonofabitch, was a movie producer who specialized in pictures with titles like *The Disemboweled Milkmaid* and like that. Pictures where teen-age girls were murdered with chain saws and stuff. She said she took the bastard for all he was worth, which was considerable. But it seems to me that all she ever did with her life was spy on her neighbors. She tried to tell me about every family on the street, but I excused myself politely, and went away.

I walked across to look at the Rutledge house again. While I had been drinking tea at Mrs. Maxwell's, the mail had arrived, and, knowing all the while that Mrs. M. was probably watching my every move, I took it out of the box and checked it out. Some junk. There's always some junk. But three letters that looked pretty interesting. One was obviously a bank statement. The second was from a club in Las Vegas. *Not* one of those offers of a cheapie gambling tour, but a letter on heavy paper. I jotted down the bank branch and the name of the Vegas club. The third envelope was the most interesting. It was addressed in longhand to Mrs. Rutledge, with no return address, postmarked "Salinas." As you know, most of Carmel's mail gets postmarked Salinas. So this was a letter from somebody up there, a personal letter to Stephanie Rutledge. Now, you wouldn't think that the lady's husband would write her a letter. Or would you? Maybe.

I stuffed the mail back in the box. I sure would have liked to swipe that last one. But I really didn't want to get into any federal trouble, you know what I mean.

After that I did some pretty tricky things. First I went to Rutledge's bank and inquired about him, representing myself as an IRS agent. Funny, they didn't even ask me for ID. They told me yes, he did have an account there. Yes, it was a checking account. And yes, it was in the low four figures. Damn! The low *four* figures. Any other accounts? No. How long? About five years. Nothing.

But then I called the Las Vegas club and inquired about Mr. Rutledge. I was switched to the office and told that he was not in at the moment, but they were expecting him. Could he call back? No, thank you. But I felt like cheering. I had something for real. Rutledge *is* connected to that club in Las Vegas. How, I don't know. But he sure as hell is known there.

On a hunch, I drove out to the Rutledge house. I didn't know why. I sat in my car about half-way down the street and waited. For what, I don't know. But in just about an hour, a car drove up the Rutledge driveway. Not really much of a car, some sort of Toyota, I think. The driver got out first, a huge man with a great drooping mustache. He seemed to swagger a little as he walked around the front end of the car and opened the door on the passenger side. He gallantly offered his hand to the passenger, a tall, beautiful blonde lady, and, grasping her elbow, escorted her to the front door. He removed the mail from the box and handed it to her. She spotted the hand-addressed envelope and smiled up at the man. He gave a short bow, and went back to his automobile. She went inside hastily. I watched the guy with the mustache drive away. Then I left.

I don't know why, but I wasn't satisfied. I went back to the house after dinner and staked it out again. I waited and waited. I was just about ready to call it quits, when another car pulled up in the driveway, a big silver Jaguar sedan. The guy that got out was *not* Harrison Rutledge, at least not the way he was described to me. It was certainly *not* Eric Farnham. This was a big, prosperous-looking stud, with an expensive suit and a self-confident attitude. He rang the bell and immediately was let into the house by, I guess, Mrs. Rutledge.

Two more things. I didn't know it until now, but one of my cousins is a lieutenant on the Glendale police. Sab Morita. I really chewed Charlotte out for not telling me right away. It could have saved me a lot of trouble. Maybe. Sab was on vacation, though, so I didn't get to talk to him. The other thing is, I checked out all the decent restaurants on Cahuenga. Yes, Farnham worked at one of them for a while, but left under very peculiar circumstances. He had acquired a bunch of steady customers, guys who asked for him every time they came in. He always seemed to talk to them more than was necessary to take their order. He even sat down with them on occasion. Then, one day he just didn't show up for work. They couldn't get in touch with him. He had given them a phony address, and the telephone number turned out to be a pay phone on Lankershim Boulevard. Just disappeared into thin air. About a week ago.

I think we ought to get in touch with Sab Morita. He's supposed to be back Monday. I *know* he'll be able to help.

I'm returning $657 to our bank account. I really didn't have to take Charlotte and her husband to dinner, because her husband was on a business trip to Chicago, and she had to stay home every evening to take his phone call. The car didn't cost much, and I decided not to do any shopping. Hope this report is OK.

14

Despite her insistence, I would not take off my underwear.

ALL OF THE above was set down on lined yellow paper in the painfully neat handwriting of my partner, the *sansei* lady. A lot of it, of course, was chatty and irrelevant, but among the nuggets of information were a few that would provide us some significant leads.

Saturday afternoon Reiko had helped me get my things together and check out of Community Hospital. They didn't ask me for any money, but said cheerfully that they'd send me a bill. I was damned sure they would.

My right arm was still in sort of a sling, and it was no little trick to get into Reiko's Honda Civic, a newish vehicle for which she had tearfully sacrificed her old Mustang. As a matter of fact, when I finally got out of bed, I discovered a number of small aches and pains I didn't think I had ever had before. But then, those of us of a certain age learn to live with small aches and pains.

The most disturbing thing to a man in his fifties is that he tends to think any small ache or pain is an indication of the onset of his terminal illness.

Reiko helped me out of her car at my house (George's house) at Sixth and Santa Rita in Carmel. She even insisted on helping me up

51

the narrow staircase to the bedroom and putting me to bed. Despite her insistence, I would not take off my underwear.

"There are some things that must remain personal, Reiko," I said, gravely. "You and I have always had a nice close business relationship, and it would never be the same if you see my nakedness."

"Shit!" she said. "I remember a time when you carried me up to my apartment, undressed me, put on my nightie, and put me to bed. You sure as hell saw *my* nakedness."

I remembered that night with some pleasure, I am ashamed to say. Reiko had fallen into a deep sleep on the way home, and I did put her to bed. I did lust mightily, I will confess. But, being the gentle soul that I am, I resisted the impulse to—well, just resisted. Reiko has meant a lot to me. I'm pretty possessive about her. But I've never given in to my baser urges where she is concerned. Although I cannot imagine why. She seems so—so *miniature* alongside Sally Morse. Perfect, but *miniature*.

"Yes, I remember. And it was quite an experience. But you, my dear, are young and supple. I am old and baggy. You know I won't wear swim trunks any more."

"Why is it you've never put a move on me? Do I just turn you off, or something?"

"Lord no, small one. It's just that I—that I—well, you know. You're like a *daughter* to me." I lied. Reiko would never be like a daughter to me. But I realized long ago that, even though I had always been just a little bit in love with her, anything more than just a hug, or a peck on the cheek, was out of the question. Early in our relationship, I had hinted about marriage. But as long as her mama was alive, she would refuse marriage to a non-Japanese. Even though she currently appeared to be involved with my old friend Greg Farrell, a shaggy artist type from Big Sur.

At just that moment I heard the door slam downstairs and a heavy step on the stairs. In seconds, Farrell burst through the door with a wild look in his eye.

"Jesus, what happened to you? I just heard you were in the hospital. When I went over there they told me you'd gone home. I ran into Tony Balestreri down at Safeway and he said you'd been shot. Why didn't you call me, you dumb bastard?" Then, to Reiko: "Hello, honey, where've you been. I called you Thursday, Friday and this morning. Are you hiding from me?"

"I'm glad you're here, Greg," she said. "Get this moose out of his skivvies and into his nightshirt. He refuses to let me see his private parts." And she went downstairs.

"Hey, wait. You didn't tell me where you'd been." I could hear her throaty laugh floating up from the living room.

"She was on a mission, Greg. For the company. It's a case that has roots down in Glendale." That seemed to pacify him for the moment. He helped me off with my underwear and into my nightshirt.

"Jesus, Pat. First, you get a bullet from God knows who. Next thing you know, Reiko will be out somewhere and get shot. I thought you only took cases that couldn't possibly involve violence or bloodshed. Please let me lend you one of my guns. I've got a little automatic down at the house that would suit you just fine. You could carry it in a holster under your coat, and nobody would ever know. And you know damn well you can get a permit."

"Greg, I'm not being noble about this, but I will *not* carry a gun. You know why. You were in Viet Nam. You saw as much bloodshed as I did, or more. You choose to keep weapons. I don't. I respect you. You respect me. Let's leave it at that."

Living in the wilderness as he does, Greg probably needs the protection of a gun. His little canyon down Highway One was used at one time for growing marijuana by a community of hippies. There's still a lot of cannabis cultivated in those canyons down there, back in hidden crevices. And you can never be too sure nor too safe.

When I finally got to bed in my own little house, I fell immediately into a deep sleep. Exhaustion had caught up with me Those nights in the hospital under sedation had kept me more or less out of it, but nobody really sleeps in a hospital. The noises are too much. The night crew seems always to be having a little party around the nurse's station. Loud laughter prevails among those people who have just come on after a day's sleep. They're all so goddam glad to see each other, and they have so much to talk about.

As I drifted off, I suddenly remembered that I had told Farnham I'd be in the office Saturday afternoon. But at that moment I couldn't have cared less. He'd find me.

When I awoke, it was dark outside, and the aroma of food wafted up from downstairs. Reiko appeared in my door, as if knowledge of my awakening had somehow been telegraphed to her.

"You awake?" she asked, perfectly aware that I was sitting on my bed trying to get my bony feet into my slippers. "Let me help you downstairs. I've fixed up a few things I found in the kitchen. 'Course, I had to run down to Bruno's for some meat. I'll pan broil you a nice filet mignon. You *are* hungry, aren't you?"

"Where's Greg?"

"Oh, he had to go down to the Art Association. He's supposed to help hang a show. He didn't want to go, but I shooed him off."

I made my way across the Mexican tiles on the living room floor, and sat down heavily on the only easy chair in the room.

"Call me when you're ready, my love."

"In a jif. You don't want this meat too well done, do you?"

Sitting back in the chair, I tried to make my right arm and shoulder as comfortable as possible. I really didn't want to get up when the phone rang.

Reiko bustled in and grabbed the telephone. "Riordan's residence. Moshi-moshi." In a moment she turned to me. "It's Tony. Something important."

The phone cord is fortunately long enough to reach the easy chair. She handed it to me.

"What's up, Tony?"

"You're not going to believe this. We got an anonymous call telling us that something was going on at the Rutledge house on the Point. When our cruiser got there, the only person on the premises was Harrison Rutledge himself. And he was deader than a doornail. On the floor. In the living room. Face down, with his hands tied behind his back. Two twenty-two slugs in the back of the head. Execution style. Any ideas?"

15

"Rutledge is dead."

IT'S A KIND of a strange feeling, know what I mean? Here I am, wounded and temporarily out of action, hearing of the death of a guy about whom I know very little, and feeling some sort of genuine shock. Harrison Rutledge was nothing to me, really. He was a name. Somebody who bought Felicia Montalvo's house on Carmel Point. Had a wife who apparently had a thing for other men, including the client I had accepted reluctantly for a lousy $5,000. Aw, come off it, Riordan, you needed the money for the office rent.

But I *would* have liked to meet the guy. I mean how can you *really* evaluate a suspicious character if you don't face-to-face the sonofabitch. Suddenly, I was angry because Rutledge had the gall to get himself killed before I could question him.

"Hey. Where the hell are you?" Balestreri was shouting in my ear. I was sitting there grinding my teeth and not saying anything.

"Sorry. Slow reactions, Tony. What happens when you are old and traumatized. You're sure it was Rutledge?"

"Sure as we can be without an eyeball identification. Stuff in his pockets says he was Rutledge. Fits the general description. White male, maybe five-nine, 145 pounds, glasses. Gotta wait 'til the wife gets up here. My people are trying to get hold of her in Glendale. Hey, this is strange. Seems they still own a house down there. This one and the other one. Takes a bunch of loot to manage that, right?"

"I know. Reiko just got back from L.A. She picked up a few tid-bits. Anything besides ID on the body? Any letters or papers or something?"

"Nada. Wallet with about $500 in it. Credit cards. Automobile insurance card. Medical insurance card. Oh, and a business card."

"Rutledge's?"

"No, somebody named Fred Giurlani. A CPA in Los Angeles. You got a connection for that one?"

"Sorry. Did you say you got hold of the wife?"

"Not yet. Phone doesn't answer. We'll keep trying. By the way, how are you feeling?"

"Rotten. Just as I thought we were getting close to this guy, somebody kills him. Execution style, you say?"

"Couldn't have been any neater. The man's ankles were tied, hands tied behind the back. He was probably made to assume the kneeling positon and dispatched with the two slugs at close range. I meant how do you feel physically?"

"My neck hurts, my shoulder hurts, my arm is still in a sling and somebody has to cut my meat for me. And now I'm depressed. Thanks for the call. If you find the wife or anything else comes up, call me. *Especially* if you get hold of the wife."

We said our perfunctory good-byes. Reiko took the phone from me and put in back on the cradle. Then she turned and put her hands on her hips.

"Rutledge is dead. Shot in his living room by a hit man. Right?"

"Yeah. I think your trip down South may have been a waste of time, honey. We're back to square one. When did you say your Glendale cop cousin gets back?"

"Monday. I'll call him early in the morning. Or maybe at his home Sunday night. Charlotte gave me his number."

I could not help wondering where Farnham was. He'd probably show up professing complete innocence of Rutledge's shooting. And with a solid alibi.

"Ready for your filet?" said Reiko.

"Oh, sure. On the rare side, please. I'm beginning to get hungry."

We ate in silence at the little table in the kitchen. Reiko had found some frozen lima beans and a reasonably fresh tomato for salad. It was not the greatest meal I ever had, but it beat hell out of hospital food. At least, the steak was great.

After dinner, while Reiko was washing the dishes, I lay down on the couch in the living room. The radio was going in the kitchen. One of those interminable talk shows during which people craving some sort of recognition call up to discuss their theories for world peace or their own tiny, often neurotic problems. These programs are usually presided over by a personality with a rich, resonant voice, and an inflated ego. Reiko loves 'em. She talks back to the people and scoffs at the omniscient host.

I couldn't understand anything that was being said on the radio. Until the station broke for news on the hour. Then I sat up and listened:

"The Monterey County Sheriff's Office reports an apparent murder on Carmel Point. The victim has been identified as Harrison Rutledge, found shot execution-style on the floor of his living room. Mr. Rutledge was a comparative newcomer to the Carmel area, having moved with his family to the Carmel Point residence only just over two years ago. The positive identification of the body was made by Rutledge's stepson, Jason Andrews, who had been visiting friends in Monterey at the time of his stepfather's death. Twenty-one year old Andrews has been in attendance at Princeton University, but had returned to the Peninsula only a day or so ago to, in his words, 'attend to some personal business.' We'll report any further developments on this story as the facts are known."

I yelled in to Reiko. "Call Balestreri. Get the bastard on the phone. Why didn't he tell me about the kid?"

"It isn't *my* case. And stop yelling at me." The Sergeant was a little pissed off when I reached him. "I gave you all I knew. How was I to know that the kid had showed up? I'm here in the office. All I know is what they tell me. What I get is that the kid came in the door about a half hour after the cruiser got there, and identified the corpse. They've asked him to hang around and they're bringing him in for questioning tomorrow morning. Now, are you satisfied?"

"Sorry, buddy. I really didn't think you were holding out on me. Call me tomorrow, will you?"

Deep down, I really did think he had been holding out on me, but I wasn't going to tell him that. "Turn the goddam radio off," I yelled at Reiko. She did, and for a few minutes all I could hear was the sound of the washing of dishes.

At length, she came into the living room and sat primly in one of the occasional chairs, saying nothing.

"Why are you staring at me?" I asked.

"You're getting back to normal, aren't you? Shouting at me as usual. Forgetting that I'm your partner, not your handmaiden. You can be a bit of a shit sometimes, Riordan."

I apologized. "Come over here and sit." I scrunched up and made a place for her on the couch. She sat beside me and I put my arm around her. "I'm sorry, little one. Please don't mention this to Sally, but I love you. Really. I've never said that to you before. But it's true. I'm not sure just what kind of love it is. I just know what I feel right now."

"It's the demerol. Stays in your system, they say. You're still a little goofy. But I love you, too."

And she kissed me on the bald spot. There is not much electricity transmitted through a bald spot, but I got a nice warm feeling.

"Do you suppose if I help you upstairs you can take care of yourself tonight? So I can go home and unpack and take a bath and get some rest myself?"

"I'll be just fine. But promise me one thing. Come back early in the morning, and pick up some bagels on the way. I know I'll sleep, but I kind of doubt I can handle breakfast."

I made it up the stairs without much help. Since the bed hadn't been made up since I slept in it last, I just slid in. Reiko patted me on the arm and tiptoed out the door. I heard her go down the stairs. The coat closet creaked as she got out her jacket. The front door groaned as she opened it. And then I heard voices.

"Is this the residence of Patrick Riordan, the private investigator?" I recognized the slight Hispanic inflections of Angel Garcia. "I have business with him. Is he able to see me for a few minutes?"

"Well, if it's urgent," said Reiko. "I don't think he's asleep yet. Who's this?"

"Oh, I am sorry, señorita. This is the son of the lady for whom I am making an investigation. Mr. Riordan knows my problem. I did not get your name. But please meet Mr. Jason Andrews. Miss . . . ?"

"Masuda. Mr. Riordan's partner. Just back from Glendale. Hi, Mr. Andrews. I feel I know you already."

16

"Come on, Jason, and shut up,"
said Angel Garcia.

JASON ANDREWS was what almost everybody would recognize as a 21-year-old junior at Princeton. The clothes were stylishly baggy. Why is it that all the fashion-conscious young men wear clothes that look like hand-me-downs? The shoulders droop, the pants are pleated and ballooning, the sleeves are too long—and that's what they *want* to wear. Looks like the sax section of the Glenn Miller band. I'd rather see the old Brooks Brothers look. But, what the hell, I'm no arbiter of haute couture. My usual costume is jeans, running shoes, a plaid shirt unsullied by a tie, and sometimes an old tweed jacket with frazzled elbows. It's the kind of garment that cries out for leather patches, but it seems nobody makes 'em anymore.

Jason and Angel Garcia stood at the foot of my bed expressionless. I peered up at them through half-closed eyes, cunningly trying to give the impression that I was weak from my wound and under sedation. At least, I thought I was being cunning. Garcia boomed out in a loud clear voice:

"Mr. Riordan, this is the son of my client. You are associated with Eric Farnham. My client's son is of the opinion that Mr. Farnham killed his stepfather. He tells me that Mr. Farnham had some dealings with his stepfather that led to very bad feelings. Can you enlighten us as to the whereabouts of Mr. Farnham?"

I could no longer feign chemically induced stupor. I sat up in bed abruptly and glared at Garcia.

"You have deliberately confused the issue here, Angel. What you told me when we first met was that this young fellow's mother hired you to find Farnham because of a busted romance. Now you say the kid thinks Farnham killed Rutledge. What was the connection? What's the real story?"

Garcia shrugged. "A ruse, Mr. Riordan. Mrs. Rutledge had other reasons to locate Farnham. She did not tell me everything. But those other reasons involved a great deal of money. That is why Mr. Andrews is here."

I looked again at Jason Andrews. He was probably six feet tall, slender in his baggy clothes, and had a pasty face to match his almost colorless hair. In the poor light of my bedroom I could almost see the pale fringe of an unsuccessful mustache on his upper lip. When he spoke, his voice had a nasal quality, and his inflections were those of a rather petulant adolescent.

"I don't know why Mr. Garcia is being so polite with you. We know you work for Farnham. It's necessary that we interface with him ASAP, understand? The man is programmed to kill people. And you know where he is, don't you?" The young man's eyes flashed for a second and then returned to dullness. He seemed ready to stamp his foot.

"Item one, I do not know where Farnham is. Item two, if I did know, I wouldn't tell you. Item three, I've got a bullet hole in me and, despite the pain it would undoubtedly cause me, if you remain in my face, I will rise from this bed and flatten your aristocratic nose. Do I make myself clear?"

Garcia threw out an arm and pushed young Andrews to the background. "Please forgive the young man, Mr. Riordan. It is just that he is overwrought over the death of his stepfather. I see now that it was a mistake to come here tonight. Perhaps in the morning. Or later tomorrow. We will take our leave now." He grasped Jason Andrews by the arm with authority, and led him out of the room and down the stairs.

Over his shoulder, the young man threw me a malevolent glare. "You have much to answer for, sir. And I intend to get to the. . . ."

"Come on, Jason, and shut up," said Angel Garcia.

Reiko glided into the room.

"I heard. I was in the bathroom. What do you make of this development? Adds to the confusion, doesn't it?"

"Honey, I am very tired and I hurt to my toes. But I am convinced of one thing. What Garcia told me in the beginning was for real. Farnham *was* having a thing with Stephanie Rutledge. Maybe this creepy kid didn't know about it, but my gut instinct says it's true. On the other hand, there must have been some connection between Farnham and Rutledge. Farnham has been lying through that big grin of his about that. Goddamit, why am I always surrounded by liars and thieves?"

"You are in the business of private investigation, dummy. Very few people are going to tell you the whole truth. Here, take a pill and go to sleep."

She took a plastic phial from my dresser and tapped out a capsule. Grasping my nose with thumb and forefinger, she popped the thing in my mouth. Then, before I could object, she poured half a tumbler of water down my throat. In about fifteen minutes, I fell into a dreamless sleep.

Bright sunlight woke me. Confused, I looked at the window and swore softly to myself because I had forgotten to pull the drape. Then I looked at the clock, trying to focus on its digital readout from across the room. 8:45 it said. A.M. or P.M.? Must be morning 'cause night ain't bright like that, I thought, amused at my clumsy paraphrase. The smell of bacon and coffee rose up the stairwell from the kitchen. I sat up gingerly and was surprised that I felt much stronger than I had the night before. I pulled on an old bathrobe that should have been retired years ago, and made my way downstairs.

Sally Morse was in the kitchen moving efficiently from stove to sideboard to table and back, as if she were actually used to cooking. "I thought I heard you. It's Sunday morning, darling, and I'm here for the day. Anything special you want to eat. I just fixed myself some bacon and eggs." She kissed me affectionately, taking care not to disturb my right shoulder. "Reiko called me last night and said you needed me. That's unusual for her, isn't it? Sometimes I think she's convinced that she *owns* you. But she said you needed what I could give you. What did she mean by that?"

"Want to go back up to bed?" I said, trying to look innocent.

"Hold it, Riordan. You're not back in shape yet. Let's give it a few days, anyhow."

"OK. Bacon and eggs. Eggs over easy. Some toast and marmalade. Whatever." Sally must have brought the groceries with her. I never keep bacon around, and I treat myself to about an egg a week. A young doctor of my acquaintance insisted a while back that I go through an ultrasound on the carotid arteries and said that if I didn't lay off the fats and other dangerous foodstuffs, I'd have to have my plumbing rooted out. I've been reasonably good ever since.

"I hear you had visitors last night. Hell of a time to drop in, wasn't it?" She was expertly flipping my eggs with a plastic spatula.

"Sal, I have never been involved in such a complicated mess in my life."

"That's got to be an exaggeration, sport. You seem *always* to be involved in complicated situations. Or do you just complicate 'em yourself?"

"Are you still serious about me going into the travel business?"

"Any time."

I thought about that for a long moment. Me, a travel agent. Making airline reservations for rich people. Scheduling tours for senior citizen groups. Na-a-a-ah.

"Forget it. I am what I am. An old dog. Goddam, that hurt." I had forgetfully tried to rest my right elbow on the table. "Sally, will you marry me?"

"No. Here's your bacon and eggs. Shut up and eat."

After breakfast I told her about the visit of the night before from Garcia and the young snot Andrews. "They might come back again this morning. Tell 'em I have fallen into a swoon, and am babbling in tongues, or something. I don't want to see that obnoxious kid again."

At almost that precise moment, somebody agitated the wrought iron knocker on the front door.

"What do I do, Pat?" Sally looked at me with raised eyebrows.

"Answer it," I said, wearily. "It might be United Parcel."

But it wasn't. It was Angel Garcia. He smiled at Sally. "I am sorry to intrude, señorita. But may I see Mr. Riordan. I am alone, if he asks."

"Let him in, Sal."

I heaved my aching body out of the wooden chair in the kitchen, and made my way into the living room. With studied nonchalance, I draped my body on the couch.

"Now, Angel, what can I do for you? And why did you bring that skinny college boy with you last night?"

"It was at his insistence, Mr. Riordan. He is an impetuous youth. We met at the Rutledge house. I had gone there to find my client. He was taking charge of the premises after his stepfather's death."

"Well, did you find Mrs. Rutledge?"

"That is my dilemma, Mr. Riordan. She is not to be found, either in Carmel or Glendale. I have called her private number and I have sent my operatives to her door. She seems to have vanished altogether."

17

"Much of what I told you was true."

Angel Garcia stood in the middle of my living room, a formidable presence. He was well over six feet tall and weighed at least 240. The mustache gave him the look of a latter day Pancho Villa, but at that moment, in my house, he looked bewildered and unhappy.

I looked at Sally. "Upstairs, on my bedside table you'll find a sheaf of yellow legal paper with a lot of small imitation Japanese writing on it. Get it for me, like a good girl." She went up the stairs obediently. I'm sure it was the first time in our relationship that Sally ever did anything I asked her to do without question. Gives a guy a ray of hope.

"Angel, my associate spent some time in Glendale last week. What I just sent the lady for is her report. I will show it to you. You may read it at your leisure. But one thing I will tell you before you read. Stephanie Rutledge was at home entertaining a visitor as recently as Friday night. My associate was unable to identify the man who knocked on her door, but she describes him, as I recall, as a 'big, prosperous-looking stud.' *And* earlier that same day, my associate tells me, the lady was escorted to her door by a large gentleman with a mustache who looked a hell of a lot like you, Angel. She further determined that Harrison Rutledge was importantly connected to a fairly large casino in Las Vegas. Now, what do you think of that?"

Sally arrived with Reiko's report as Garcia sank into my only easy chair and covered his face with large hairy hands.

"I should have known. Sergeant Balestreri told me that you are a shrewd and experienced investigator. I should have known that you would have someone examining the background of the Rutledge family. I suppose you know about Lisa, also."

"Who's Lisa, for God's sake?" In my invalid state I was not so patient and temperate as I think I would have been ordinarily.

"Ah, you do not know about Lisa. It is now time for me to tell you the entire story, Mr. Riordan. Lisa Andrews is Jason's sister, the daughter of Mrs. Rutledge. There was a fiction invented to cover her absence from home. She was said to be attending an expensive women's college in the East. However, nobody, not even her mother, knows where she is.

"But let me begin from the beginning. The late Mr. Rutledge was indeed a partner in the Las Vegas establishment. He was a single man until only a few years ago when he met and married Stephanie, then only recently the widow of the children's father, Harold Andrews, a Texas oil person who made frequent trips to Nevada to feed his gambling habit. Jason and Lisa were in their late teens at the time, so Rutledge made no attempt to adopt them. Jason hated his stepfather with a passion, despite the display he made here last night. His stepfather, however, bore him no malice, and was happy to send the boy to Princeton. 'Just getting him out of here was enough,' he used to say.

"I became associated with the Rutledges early in their marriage. I had done some confidential work for certain attorneys in Glendale who recommended me to Rutledge for, let us say, important errands. Therefore, it did not surprise me when Mrs. Rutledge called me to perform certain duties for *her*. I'm sorry, Mr. Riordan, that I was not entirely forthcoming with you when we met. Much of what I told you was true. Stephanie Rutledge did hire me to find Eric Farnham, with whom she had had an unfortunate love affair. Farnham had worked for her husband at one time, and had returned to him with a tale of the great hidden wealth of a woman here in Carmel. Rutledge was furious when Farnham showed up. It seems the man had stolen from him as well as other Las Vegas operators, and was under sentence of death before receiving the protection of the local woman. I have since found out that she was indeed very powerful . . . and very rich."

The big man sat with his hands on his massive thighs, talking slowly, as much to the room as to me. Sally sat quietly beside me on the couch, taking it all in.

"But you know of what happened here, of course. When the woman was killed in a strange accident, Farnham disappeared, only to return to the Monterey Peninsula last week. Sergeant Balestreri was kind enough to tell me about you, and now we are here, in the same boat, so to speak."

I was beginning to squirm around on the couch. I do not like to sit for any length of time, listening to somebody else.

"What boat is that, Angel? The one up the creek without a paddle? I foolishly took a job for a crook because I needed the money. So far, I have not done a goddam thing for him because somebody shot me. All the rest of this stuff is very interesting but irrelevant. Why should I give a damn about Harrison Rutledge or his stepkids or their romantic mama?"

Garcia smiled. "Because you are an investigator, Mr. Riordan. Investigators who are worth anything at all are always eager to follow up an interesting case. *And* because I have a very strong suspicion that it was Lisa Rutledge who shot you."

18

"A pretty face, although it has a look of danger."

I COULD NOT HELP wondering why a young woman whose existence I had not even known about three minutes ago, would try to kill me. Sometime in the dim and distant past (not quite a week ago, actually), *somebody* told me that Rutledge had two kids. One of them had materialized in my bedroom only recently. But my large Latino friend was sitting there smiling, telling me that he thought the other Rutledge offspring had shot me. For reason or reasons yet unknown.

"Angel . . . Angel, tell me why you think this Lisa would want to dispose of me."

"That I do not know, Mr. Riordan. But when the young woman was last seen, she was driving a modified pickup truck. Many knew her to be a gun enthusiast. One of the few women I have known who is actually a member of the NRA. Always something of what your people called a 'tomboy,' you understand. Although it is not that she is known to be attracted to other girls. As a matter of fact, she has been known to cohabit with males ever since she was fourteen. Her mother told me that she returns home periodically, usually after becoming bored with her roommate. She is now nineteen and neither her mother nor her stepfather has seen her for some eighteen months.

However, she did telephone her mother quite recently, and hinted that she was living somewhere in the Monterey Bay Area with a young man who makes wrought-iron sculptures. She was unhappy, she said, because the guy constantly smelled of acetylene. Its perfume is not, I suspect, aphrodisiac."

Garcia had relaxed considerably. He lolled back in the armchair, a springless affair that encourages abominable posture, and smiled at the thought of the Mrs. Rutledge's only daughter being repelled by an oil-stained, smelly lover.

"Have you seen this girl, Angel? Can you describe her?"

"I have only seen a picture of her. When I was in the Rutledge home in Glendale. She is small, shorter than her mother. Dark blonde hair which she apparently prefers to wear very short. A pretty face, although it has a look of danger. Do you know what I mean, Mr. Riordan? There is something in the eyes. . . . But of course, the picture I saw was taken when she was seventeen or so. She may have changed a great deal since then."

"And, I suspect, not for the better. Why do you think it was she who took a shot at me? And do you think that it was Lisa also who snuck into the hospital and put a bullet in the pillow on the other bed?"

"It is what you call a hunch. Lisa must have found out why her father had been so eager to buy the house on Carmel Point. You understand, of course, that he had been convinced by Farnham that Felicia Montalvo's fortune must have been hidden there somewhere. Or, at least, that there could be found some clue in the house. Rutledge did not hesitate to buy the house. He had never even seen it. He and his wife filled it with expensive furnishings and spent only weekends in it for the better part of two years. Rutledge discreetly tried to become a member of the community. He gave money to local charitable organizations. He even tried to join the Cypress Point Golf Club, although the members turned him down rather quickly. Somebody has to die, you know. Rutledge was truly injured by that. He had never had any trouble in Southern California buying what he wanted. One day he swore to me that he would make an offer to Marvin Davis for all of Pebble Beach. But it never came to pass."

"I'm sure you've got lots of interesting stories, and that you tell them very well, but for God's sake, get to the point. Why would Lisa Andrews want to kill me?"

Garcia smiled his warm, sweet smile again. "Oh, I don't think Lisa wanted to kill you, Mr. Riordan. But she must have found out that you were working for Farnham, and she wanted to frighten you away. This is the way I have put it together: Her mother told Lisa that Rutledge had bought the Carmel house because of the fortune it was said to contain. Lisa, who was living somewhere north of here in a place called Aptos, decided to conduct a search on her own. Either she ran into Farnham, whom she might have known from earlier contacts, or she saw him at the house. She must have followed him, connected him with you. Upon learning of your reputation as an investigator, she decided to try to eliminate you from the picture. Does that make sense?"

My shoulder was beginning to hurt like hell. And the Rutledge-Andrews family was assuming the character of a sort of evil situation comedy. There was very little—if any—love or loyalty of one to another. Harrison Rutledge was lucky to be out of it. He was dead. Mama was not to be found for the moment. The son was sort of an ivy-school crybaby. And the daughter uninhibited and dangerous. Not your Cosbys or your "Family Ties" group.

"I have another question, Angel. This prosperous looking hunk that my operative saw entering the Rutledge house in Glendale. Any idea?"

Garcia sighed. "I am sure it was Eddie Colucci, one of the partners in the Las Vegas casino. Your fellow Farnham has not been the only gentleman enjoying the favors of Stephanie Rutledge. And, although it is perhaps ungallant to say it, the number was not restricted to *two*."

"You're saying that Stephanie liked to sleep around, right? But you don't know where she is now. She might be in Las Vegas. She might be anywhere in the L.A. basin. She might be at Disneyland, for that matter. Angel, you tell a great story, but I don't think you're such a hot detective. I think it's time for you to leave, now. I'm very tired, and I want my lady friend here to take me up and put me to bed. You can take down the number on the telephone if you want to get in touch. I keep forgetting it because I never call it. Now, if you will just not let the door handle hit you in the ass as you go out. . . ."

"I will keep in touch, Mr. Riordan." The big man hauled himself reluctantly out of the chair. "Please do the same for me. I am staying at the Casa Munras in Monterey. By the way, can you recommend a good place to eat near there. Reasonable, of course. I have not the unlimited expense account. And, please, *not* Mexican. Very few restaurants know how to prepare Mexican food."

"The Clock Garden. On Abrego. Get the early dinner. It's enough even for a big guy like you. The food is better at Casanova which is just a few blocks from here, but the tables are too close together, and the prices are pretty steep. Go to the Clock."

On his way out, Garcia picked up a white sombrero from a table near the door. I hadn't seen him wear a hat up to this moment, and wasn't aware that he had been wearing one when he came in. He clapped the thing on his head and tugged it down. "Out of respect for my heritage, Mr. Riordan," he said, anticipating my question. With the hat on he had to duck a little as he went out the door.

Sally had been mousy quiet all during my long conversation with Garcia. It wasn't like her. She sat with her arms folded, staring into space.

"Well, Sal, what did you think of all that?"

She turned slowly to me. "Is this what you do all the time? You know what I do. But does this happen often? I mean, characters like that coming to your house and telling you all kinds of unbelievable stories. You make a living at this?"

"You can see I am not rolling in wealth, my dear. Yes, these things happen. Yes, people tell me outlandish stories. I'm supposed to apply my built-in bullshit strainer, and separate out the nuggets of truth. Or, at least, the nuggets that might be of some help, even if they aren't the truth."

"What can happen next?" she asked, frowning.

"The next person I expect to come through that door will be . . . well, either Stephanie Rutledge *or* Lisa Andrews."

A fierce pounding came from the old rusty knocker on my door. "There, I told you, Sally. Everything comes to him who waits. Get the door for me. There's a good girl."

Sally opened the door a crack and was immediately blasted back into the room by a small but determined figure wearing a leather outfit like something I have only seen in catalogues of erotic material that somebody keeps sending me. Some of 'em are pretty interesting. But I had never seen a garment like this on a real woman, let alone in my own living room. Especially a woman who filled it so beautifully. Especially a nineteen-year-old girl with blazing eyes who I knew instantly was Lisa Andrews.

19

"He'd rub up against me any chance he got."

THE GIRL STOOD in the middle of the room and glared in silence. I took the opportunity to get a good look at her. She was, as Garcia had suggested, a little wild-eyed. Maybe that's understating it. She was mad as hell, and she wasn't going to take it any more. You know, like the guy in the movie. The leather pants might have been applied with Crazy Glue, and the jacket (I don't know what else to call it) fitted the contours with considerable pleasure. There was about a three inch space between the two pieces that allowed examination of her navel, and I was mildly surprised that there wasn't a small skull and crossbones imbedded in it. Her head was bare, and her hair stood out like Elsa Lanchester's after Dr. Frankenstein threw the switch.

"Aren't you cold in that outfit?" was all that I could think of to say. After all, it was hard onto mid-October, and there was a distinct chill in the air.

She snorted and bared her teeth. "That fat sonofabitch Garcia was here, wasn't he? Don't lie to me. I saw him leave. What kind of bullshit did he try to feed you? Did he tell you about me?"

"Kindly identify yourself, dear. Only then will I be able to answer your questions. You seem a bit overwrought."

"I think you know goddam well who I am. I think you know all

71

about my whole goddam family. For the book, I am Lisa Andrews. Garcia told you I tried to kill you, didn't he? Well, it's a big stinking lie. Garcia is a . . ."

She went on with a string of unflattering references to the East L.A. detective that I choose not to reproduce here. Let us just say that she made allusions to the strangeness of the man's sexual orientation and that she ended with a favorite Latin American insult in twelve letters that involved the man's relationship with his mother. For those who crave more details, the operative word in Mexican-Spanish is "chingar."

I gazed in wonderment at this very pretty young girl whose vocabulary was worthy of a cross-country semi operator. Ah, one learns when one is thrust into the world untutored. But Lisa's education was hard won, and, I suspect, her demonstration in my living room that night was motivated more by her anger than her essential coarseness.

"Slow down, honey. Take a seat and let's talk this over. Don't mind my chaperone. She's just here to make me take my medicine and put me to bed." I glanced at Sally, who was staring open-mouthed at Lisa Andrews, wondering whether to mother her or punch her out.

Suddenly, Lisa looked like a little girl who got caught smoking a cigarette in the bathroom. The fury went out of her face, and she plopped down in the same chair from which Garcia had arisen only minutes before. I wondered if it was still warm.

"Let me get a grip on myself," she said. Her face, in repose, suggested a certain sadness. She tugged at the bottom of her jacket, as if suddenly aware that her midriff was bare. She tucked her legs up under her, and clasped her hands around her knees. Her hair, which had been flying around her face moments before, had relaxed and framed her face flatteringly. I could almost imagine her in a cheerleader's outfit from Carmel High.

"Ever since Mama married that man, I've tried to stay away. I was never ever happier than when I heard he was dead. He was a complete no-good, know what I mean? He was groping me when I was thirteen, even before Mama married him. Harrison Rutledge looked like a wimp. He was a skinny, scrawny little guy with glasses, but he sure was horny. He'd rub up against me any chance he got. He even tried to get me to put my hand on him, you know where." She was no longer the sharp-tongued little street girl, but had become shy and a little prudish.

"Lisa, why are you here? Oh, I can understand that the lure of Felicia Montalvo's great fortune can affect even the strongest among us. But, from what I've been told, you have been on your own for quite a while, apparently enjoying the free and easy life. I can imagine that you have more or less kept in touch with your mother, and knew about the house on Carmel Point. But following Angel Garcia around and bursting in on me. I don't understand."

"You're right about one thing. Mother gave me your name. I guess she got it from that other awful man, Eric Farnham. Actually, I was trying to bust out of a relationship with this untalented sculptor in Aptos when I called her. She had just hired Garcia to chase after Farnham, although why she got that fat slob is beyond me. He ran errands for my stepfather. She should have known he'd blab to Rutledge. I'm surprised that Rutledge didn't have Mom killed. Like I said, he was a wimpy little man, but he could be deadly."

"Lisa, did you shoot me?"

"No! No matter what that lard-ass detective told you. I suppose he told you I have a collection of target pistols and load my own. Hell, I learned to shoot when I was six. My *real* father was a Texan. He believed that everybody should know how to handle a gun. He had me on the target range once a week until he died. But I didn't shoot you. I hit what I aim at. If I'd have shot you, you wouldn't be around now. No, it wasn't me. But I've got a good notion who it was."

"*Everybody* seems to have a good notion who it was. Somebody thought it was Farnham. Garcia thought it was you. Now, who's your candidate."

"My big brother Jason. 'Big brother' is a laugh. He's a gutless wonder if there ever was one."

"Why would Jason want me dead? What kind of a threat did I present to him."

She scrunched down lower in the chair. "Oh, I don't know. But it's just the kind of thing he would do. Shoot at you and just nick you. Then lose his nerve at the hospital and fire at the wrong bed. He's such a complete zero." I was startled that Lisa knew about the "wrong bed" incident at the hospital. But I chose not to mention it.

"You're not helping me, Lisa. You followed Garcia up here. You burst in here full of anger and wonderfully colorful language. You bruised Sally, as a matter of fact, by pushing that door in on her. And you really don't know anything that's helpful. If you're looking for a father-image you came to the wrong place. If you don't have a place to sleep, you can use this couch. It makes up into a bed, but I don't have any extra sheets."

"OK. But I'm hungry. Got anything to eat?"

"There's a can of soup on that whirligig in the cabinet to the right of the sink. Or there's peanut butter and crackers."

I thought a minute. Something was nagging at me. "What do you know about Eddie Colucci, Lisa."

She turned pale, and all composure seemed to leave her.

"Where did you hear about him?"

"Let's just say his name came up in a conversation."

She measured her words carefully. "Eddie Colucci was the reason I left home. Rutledge tried to feel me up and all that. But Eddie took me to bed."

"Did you go willingly?"

"Oh, yes. Eddie was very persuasive. But don't tell my mother. He was *her* lover, too. Among others."

"Do you think he could have had anything to do with your stepfather's murder."

"Sure. Eddie was capable of anything. He was Rutledge's partner in the Las Vegas deal. But he'd worked his way up from killing people on contract."

I was really weary by this time. The old machine can accept only so much information. I signalled to Sally that I was ready to go upstairs. She let me lean on her to the bedroom, where she tucked me in. A few minutes later I heard her go down the stairs again. Later, I was only dimly aware of her slipping into bed beside me, but I knew that she was nice and warm.

20

"What stepdaughter?"

NEXT MORNING Lisa was gone, as I knew she would be. Sally woke up first and tip-toed down the stairs to whip up a pot of coffee. I roused about fifteen minutes later, managed to pull on my pants and, with a blanket around my shoulders, went to the bathroom. One of the wonderful things about this house is that there is a great view of the john from the street. For whatever reason, nobody has ever seen the need to put a drape or blind or something on the odd-shaped window that looks out on Sixth Avenue. Oh, there's a live oak tree outside that partially obscures the view. But I've had to resist the compulsion over the years to open the window and moon the traffic, perhaps for an entire day. Just a scientific experiment, you understand.

Sally appeared in the door of the bathroom. "She's gone. She ate half a loaf of bread and most of your peanut butter and took off. Here's her goodbye." Sally handed me a note scrawled on a paper napkin.

It read: "On my own. Thanks for the bed. If I find out who shot you, I'll call. Still think it was my stinking brother. But he wouldn't have had the guts to kill Rutledge."

Hastening to zip up my fly left-handed, I asked, "What day is this?"

"Monday. The sixteenth of October. Nineteen eighty-nine. A.D. What do you need to know for?"

"What time is it?"

"Almost eight. Why?"

"Reiko's still at home. I've got to call her. She didn't have anything in her report about Lisa. I wonder why?" I sort of lurched toward the door, and Sally caught me by the arm.

"Hold on, soldier. Let's get some clothes on you and *then* you can go downstairs and call."

She dragged me back into the bedroom. "You've still got your nightshirt on, you know that? Any underwear?"

"No, and get out. I can dress myself."

"Like hell you can. Sit down." She pushed me onto the bed. Then like the earth-mother that she would like to be, she clothed me gently from the skin out, against my vehement objections. Only my right arm was left alone, draped by a shirt and a heavy knit sweater. I had been instructed at the hospital to leave it in the sling for another three or four days. Why the hell do we always *have* to do what they tell us in the hospital? Mostly somebody is just covering his ass, the spectre of a malpractice suit floating over his head. But, good soldier that I am, I follow instructions to the letter.

With Sally's help, I made my way down the stairs and soon discovered that being without a usable right hand made even a touch-tone phone hard to manage. With more manual dexterity that I ever knew I possessed, I managed to punch out Reiko's number.

"H'lo," came a small voice at the other end.

"This is the senior partner. Did I get you up?"

"Yes. Are you all right? Didn't Sally take care of you? Why the hell are you calling this early?"

"It's after eight o'clock. It's not that early. Why aren't you up drinking coffee and getting ready to go to the office?"

"You know I don't drink coffee. And I'm resting from my labors of last week. Besides, how could you know on a Monday morning that I wouldn't already be on my way to the office?"

I ignored the question on the grounds of irrelevancy.

"Things happened over the weekend that you should know about. First, why didn't you mention in your report that Rutledge's step-daughter was alienated, and had been away from home for a couple of years?"

"What stepdaughter?"

"I'm surprised at you, Reiko. And disappointed. Lisa Andrews appeared here last night and swore she didn't shoot me, but her brother might have. How do you like that?"

"Whoever said this Lisa shot you? Where's she been?"

"Garcia, the L.A. detective said so, and she's been living with an unsuccessful metal sculptor in Aptos. How come you didn't know that?"

"Nobody said anything about any daughter. And if she's been away for a couple of years, maybe nobody knows it. Anyhow in Glendale. Sorry, inspector. Now get off the wire and let me go to work."

She slammed down the phone. I hadn't meant to sound nasty and demanding, but I guess I did. I'd have to remember to apologize. Take her a potted plant or something.

"What's for breakfast?" I asked Sally, who was standing over me with a hot cup of coffee.

"There was nothing unspoiled in your refrigerator except a half dozen frozen Snickers bars. The dry cereal in the cabinet had been there for weeks, and there was visible motion among the flakes when I peered into the box. I've been down to Wishart's bakery and back and, man, the pull up that hill is all that you ever said it was."

I have described the climb from Junipero Street up to Santa Rita as a lung-buster for middle-aged people. It may not be a forty-five degree slope like the one Walter Payton used to train on, but it's sufficient, 'twill serve. However, the giant pastries from Wishart's are more than enough reason to make the trip.

"Did you get a paper?"

"Of course, you slug. Paper's on the kitchen table. Drink your coffee."

I sipped from my cup the scalding black stuff that Sally had prepared. Only then did I remember that she is the world's worst cook, and that her not finding something to prepare for breakfast was not the most unfortunate thing that could have happened.

The Herald had the usual number of wire-service national and international stories on the front page. There was some local stuff inside, including the page four obits. Most of the people who die on the Monterey Peninsula seem to be eighty or over. Except suicides and accident victims. It's a healthy place to live if you can stay off the highways and aren't depressed by the fog.

Flipping through the pages of the main news section, I came to a sudden stop. A headline read, "Tearful Widow Accuses Son of Slaying." Above the story was a photograph of a lady who appeared to be indeed shedding tears, caught in the act of dabbing at them without completely concealing her face from the photographers.

She was identified as Stephanie Rutledge, widow of the late Harrison Rutledge. She was quoted as stating:

"Jason hated his stepfather. He had often threatened to kill him. I'm heartsick at the apparent fact that he carried out his threat."

With Mrs. Rutledge at the time of her statement, the story went on, was her daughter, Lisa.

A hasty call to a friend at the paper got me the information that the reporter had interviewed the woman on Saturday. That meant that nasty little Lisa had been lying to me, that Garcia had been lying to me, and that Stephanie had been in town over the weekend. Why the hell can't somebody tell the goddam truth!

21

"Oh, yes, Mr. Riordan. Mr. Garcia has told me about you."

CAN YOU DRIVE me to my office, Sal? I cannot sit around here all day moping. There are things that need to be done, although at the moment, I'm not sure what they are."

"I have my own business to run. I'll drive you to Monterey, but how will you get home?"

"Reiko can bring me home. Please, let's get out of here. Either the news story I've just read or that big cheese Danish gave me heartburn." I shoved the paper toward Sally and pointed out the article.

She gave a low whistle when she had finished the story. "So that's what Stephanie Rutledge looks like. She's gorgeous. What's she doing in bed with the likes of Eric Farnham?"

"What a great many people do in bed, even as you and I. But that's not the point. She was *here*. On the Peninsula. Over the weekend. Garcia knew it. Lisa knew it. Why does everybody lie to me? What the hell do I know that makes me a target for a trigger-happy shooter, and somebody who is important in a mish-mash of murder and intrigue, so important that he has to be lied to and fed implausible stories by impossible people?"

Sally is often gifted with clairvoyance. She doesn't know it, and she wouldn't believe me if I told her. But she offered the obvious solution: "Maybe because you're the only one—besides me and Reiko, of course—who's had any contact with Farnham. They think you know where he is, or how to get in touch with him. How about that?"

Seems sort of simple when you think of it. Somebody still unidentified shot at me either to kill me or to scare me, hard to tell which. Somebody put a slug in the other bed in my hospital room. Maybe the estranged wife of the guy who had checked out? Whose aesthetician had told her about her husband's shenanigans. N-a-a-ah. Rutledge's snotty stepson comes here with Garcia, the Zorro of detectives, and makes vague threats at me. The guy's stepdaughter spends the night in my house, lies to me about her idiot brother and eats all my peanut butter. And she had just spent the afternoon in the company of her mother, the mysterious Stephanie, whom Garcia could not locate. They might have just come out and asked me where Farnham was. I could have said, "I don't know" and that would have ended it all. If they believed me.

It's as though Eric Farnham is the key to Felicia Montalvo's treasure. And everybody knows it but maybe Eric. He talked his old enemy Rutledge into buying Felicia's house on Carmel Point. Then he had a tumble with Stephanie. Or maybe the lovemaking came first, who knows? But then Eric is off to Monterey to enlist me in his cause. I don't know anything because I haven't even been to Felicia's house yet. I was in the damn' hospital and schlepping around at home, a temporary invalid.

Sally took me to the office and even helped me up the steps. Reiko took over from there, guiding me into my office and gently depositing me in my chair.

"Stay there, sucker. Don't lift anything but the phone. Or maybe better, let me make the calls for you."

"I'll make my own goddam calls. Or maybe better, you can drive me over to Carmel Point. I've got to see somebody."

"You think you can survive the trip? You look pretty pale."

"I'll not only survive the trip, but I'll survive *you* unless you take me out there. Now."

Reiko usually does what I ask her to do. She'll bitch and moan a little. That's usual. But in the end, she's loyal. And she knows that I'm the guy in the business who has been around long enough to know what I'm doing. She'll try to overrule me on some little things. But she could see I was dead serious about wanting to go back to Carmel Point.

So we went. She has finally replaced the little fifteen-year-old Mustang that I never felt very comfortable in with a Honda Civic DX hatchback that is even *less* comfortable. And her driving style is straight out of Laguna Seca. But the trip wasn't half bad. Only twice was my heart in my mouth, and the rubber she burned couldn't have made more than three or four hundred pencil erasers.

We pulled up in front of Felicia's—Rutledge's—house at about ten o'clock. A tan Jaguar was in the driveway. I got out of the car with some serious pain, and waited for Reiko. There are no sidewalks out here, as there are none in Carmel, save in the business district. I noted with some distress that Reiko had pulled up about a foot onto the lawn. She came out of the car and walked around to me.

"You know what I just noticed? I just noticed you didn't have your seatbelt on. I would never have driven you all the way over without your seatbelt on. Why didn't you put your seatbelt on?" It was like Jean Valjean being accused of stealing a loaf of bread.

"I didn't wear the goddam seatbelt because my shoulder is very sore. I thought you knew that. But even if my shoulder weren't sore, you have no goddam business complaining about my seatbelt. Now, follow me."

She was a pace behind when I reached the door. I clanged the massive knocker one substantial clang. There was a rustling sound within. In a moment the door opened, and I got my first look at the widow Rutledge.

She smiled broadly. "Yes? Can I help you?"

"Mrs. Rutledge? I'm Pat Riordan. Maybe you've heard of me?"

"Oh, yes, Mr. Riordan. Mr. Garcia has told me about you. He tells me you have been very helpful."

So Garcia has been lying to her, too. Or maybe she's just lying to me. They're all liars, dammit.

I got hold of myself. "May we come in? It would be very helpful to me if I could ask you some questions."

She opened the door wide and stood aside. God, what a flood of memories! All of Felicia's paintings were still there, covering virtually every inch of wall space. Splendid paintings they were, too, even though I knew them to be skillful copies.

"I see you're admiring the art. We were certainly fortunate to be able to buy this house with all this wonderful art on the walls, weren't we?"

She didn't know that it was all fake, and I didn't choose to tell her. Felicia's art had fooled a lot of people. Out of perhaps ill-conceived respect to her memory, I just let it pass.

Mrs. Rutledge led us into her parlor. She was a tall woman, about as tall as Sally Morse, and about Sally's age. Her hair, however, was expertly tinted blonde, and bespoke weekly visits to the hairdresser. Her figure was slender and well-proportioned, and I could understand how a number of susceptible males had fallen under her spell. Her face was beautiful but immobile, probably under the restraint of now camouflaged scar tissue from expensive plastic surgery. One thing she still had was a smile that looked as if it, too, had been produced by one of the surgeons. It was the smile of a TV refrigerator saleslady, permanent and indelible.

"What are your questions, Mr. Riordan. But before you ask, I will say nothing about my relationship with Eric Farnham. On advice of attorney, you might say."

"Oh, I wasn't going to ask you about Farnham, Mrs. Rutledge. Only why have you decided to pin your husband's murder on poor dumb Jason, and where were you when Harrison Rutlege bit the dust?"

22

"Could it have been Eddie Colucci?"

Reiko's elbow was sharp in my ribs. She and I were sitting on what's called a loveseat, a sort of two-passenger couch, and she was letting me know that she disapproved strongly of my questions.

Stephanie Rutledge, on the other hand, did not change expression. Either my questions had not perturbed her in the least, or she *couldn't* change expression because of the tucks in her face. After a moment, she spoke:

"I don't have to answer your questions, Mr. Riordan. And I will not, if you don't mind, answer the first one. There are good reasons for me to suspect my son of murdering my husband. And my son is not 'dumb', Mr. Riordan. He has had a good many emotional problems, but he is certainly not 'dumb.' On the other hand, it's probably natural and fair that you want to know where I was when my husband was killed. I was in the company of a male friend in Glendale. Perhaps I'll have to identify him in court, but I see no reason to do so now."

"Could it have been Eddie Colucci?"

No reaction, no change of expression. "He was one of my husband's business associates. I know him. That's all I'll say."

I could feel Farnham's $5,000 running out. Why should I do any more for the sonofabitch when my involvement had already got me shot? If Felicia Montalvo's fortune was concealed on these premises, the Rutledges had probably already found it and disposed of it. At any rate, Farnham had covered the territory, and who knew it better? He had lived in the house for four or five years. He was very close to Felicia. Maybe he was sleeping with her. But then I remembered what Felicia had told me when I first met her, that she hadn't had an orgasm for twenty years. And looking at that face, with those piercing dark eyes and that magnificent Spanish nose, I believed every word she said.

Stephanie's smile was beginning to look ghoulish and bizarre to me. I guessed that she had started out her adult life as a rare and sparkling beauty, the belle of the ball, whose smile had charmed everybody but the Ashley Wilkes of her life, the one guy she wanted but couldn't get. So she picked the richest guys who came along to marry, and the roughest, most dangerous guys to sleep with. And as she grew older, she maintained her beauty artificially until not much remained but the smile, like the Cheshire Cat.

I plunged ahead, ignoring Reiko's sharp little elbow. "You speak of Jason's emotional problems. Are you willing to talk about *them?*"

"Why not? Jason was a quiet, sensitive little boy. He did not relate well to other children. I was often advised by his elementary school teachers to put him in therapy, but I thought that it was only a stage through which he would eventually pass. In junior high school, he fell in love with computers. Of course, his father bought him the very best equipment. And Jason would sit for hours in his room, as silent as ever, completely absorbed in his computer."

"Yeah, I know somebody else like that. It's kind of pitiful, isn't it?" Reiko's jab caused me to grunt with pain. Mrs. Rutledge looked at me anxiously.

"Is there anything wrong? Are you ill?"

"No, ma'am. I'm perfectly fine. Just a little . . . stitch in my side. Now, about Jason. What happened? Did he hack into your bank account or something? Did he invent a virus that screwed up the Pentagon?"

"Oh, no, Mr. Riordan. Jason would never have done anything dishonest. In high school, he simply closed himself off from the world. He got excellent grades in all his classes, but would rush home every afternoon to his computer. He seldom talked, even to me. He ignored his younger sister. And he hated his stepfather, whom he regarded as nothing more than a cheap gangster. Nothing could be further from the truth, Mr. Riordan. Harrison was a sharp businessman, but never outside the law."

"Did you have him in therapy during this time?"

"Off and on. We had him see several people recommended by our family physician, but nobody could penetrate his almost catatonic state. His high school teachers all praised his work, but their comments about his personality and social awareness were always the same. Each would invariably suggest that he be encouraged to be more open, more willing to socialize with his classmates. Some suggested sports, others quite frankly said he ought to pay more attention to girls. Please don't misunderstand. Jason is not homosexual. He is, even now, what I would call asexual. Just one of those people born without libido. Sad, isn't it?"

She almost lost that smile. She seemed to be sad in her eyes, disappointed that one of her offspring should have grown to manhood with no interest at all in sex.

"What exactly was his relationship with his stepfather?"

"Each pretended the other did not exist. Harrison sent Jason off to Princeton only because he had heard of it as a school in New Jersey. He was not an educated man, and had perhaps never heard of Stanford. Or he thought Stanford was just too close, even though it's some four hundred miles from Glendale. But he was a generous man, and he sent a substantial monthly allowance to Jason. He even financed Jason's trips to Europe and the Far East during summer vacations. During the past three years Jason was seldom home. Both he and Harrison liked it that way.

"But I got these disturbing letters from Jason. . . ." She paused, and the sadness in her eyes turned to fear. The smile remained. "But I've said too much already. I told you in the beginning that I have good reason to suspect that Jason killed my husband. I don't think I'd better say any more."

Reiko tugged at my sleeve, suggesting that it was time for us to leave. She had not entered into the conversation at all, which was pretty rare for her. She had just sat silent, grinding her elbow into my ribs during the entire interview.

"Well, thank you, Mrs. Rutledge. I appreciate your frankness. And I understand your unwillingness to say more. We'd better be going. My friend here has to go to the bathroom or something."

Reiko and I both stood up, and I got the damnedest pinch on the backside I had ever felt. The little witch must have been carrying a pair of pliers. Her message got through. I said a gracious goodbye to Mrs. Rutledge. Reiko nodded a Japanese nod and looked at me with fire in her eyes.

On the way to the car she hissed at me out of the side of her mouth. "You bastard! How could you embarrass me like that? And how could you swallow all that woman's bullshit?"

"What bullshit?"

"Everything she told you was a lie. You got me good when you called my attention to the fact that I hadn't found out about Lisa. But I *did* get a lot of dope about Jason that I didn't think was worth putting in my report. Jason was no recluse, and he certainly wasn't celibate. He laid every girl who would have him, and he got three of them pregnant. The only thing his mother disapproved of was that he came home one time from Princeton with the clap. Would you like to hear more?"

23

"They keep lying, Reiko."

I THINK IT WAS Ananias in the Bible who was the habitual liar, wasn't it? Who begat Baron Munchausen, who begat Major Hoople, who begat the Fusco Brothers. Maybe it was my weakness from loss of blood or the residual effect of simple trauma, but I felt dizzy.

"Take me home, sport," I said to Reiko. "I don't think I can make it through the day in the office. You can take the day off, too. No use you goin' back to Monterey to sit at that goddam computer all day."

We drove from Carmel Point to Santa Lucia, up to Dolores and thence by Eighth Avenue and Junipero up to Sixth and Santa Rita. Doesn't sound like much of a trip unless you consider speeding cars, driven by locals, concealed behind huge growths of foliage at every unmarked street corner. A short trip in Carmel is enough to stir up the adrenalin. There's a four-way stop now at my corner, where there had been nothing before. Sixth Avenue is a favorite route downtown for people in the know, and they used to start at Carpenter and sail unimpeded down to the stop sign at Torres. Some of 'em even stopped at the stop sign. But there used to be at least one fender-bender a day outside my kitchen window. This often was the cue for the entire Carmel Police Force to gather, measuring skid marks and directing traffic. Since the four-way was installed, I haven't even heard a promising screech of brakes. I sort of miss the excitement.

Anyway, we rode in silence back to my house, where Reiko pulled up on the dirt behind the kitchen door and stopped. She came around and opened the passenger door for me and carefully protected my scalp as I squeezed out.

When we got inside, I flopped down on the couch and just lay there for a while. I was barely aware of Reiko moving about in the kitchen.

"What do you think?" I heard her say. "Can the Giants come back? They sure haven't looked very good so far."

"What?"

"The Giants. Can they come back after losing two in Oakland? You know. The World Series."

I am not much of a baseball fan. Football has always been my game. I live for the autumn, and sports cease for me after the Super Bowl. But I knew that Reiko was a red-hot Dodger rooter, and really didn't care whether the Giants came back or not.

"You've been watching the Giants lose and enjoying it, haven't you? Well, I couldn't care less what they do. Are they playing today?"

"You're really out of it, aren't you. No, they're not playing today. They play tomorrow night. At Candlestick. You ought to pay more attention. You sure know when the 49ers win or lose. That's *such* a bloody, brutal game." I wasn't looking at her, but I could *hear* her shudder.

"Honey, the World Series is not the most important thing in *my* world at the moment. Besides, in a few years, the Japanese will want to be in the World Series, and *then* who you gonna root for? Please let me rest."

"Here, I fixed you a cup of tea. Sit up and drink it."

I sat up obediently. The tea was scalding hot and burned my tongue. But I had to drink it. She would have given it to me in an enema if I hadn't.

The strong tea was a tonic, though. I began to feel better. My head was clearing. And anger replaced my feeling of helplessness.

"They keep lying, Reiko. Everybody lies about everybody else. I can't believe anything I hear. Any suggestions?"

She sat down on the couch beside me and, looking very calm and confident, said: "Let's just see what we both have heard and try to pick out the truth. There's got to be some truth in all those lies."

Reiko settled back and closed her eyes. "I've got a theory about why Mrs. Rutledge tried to incriminate Jason. Want to hear it?"

"Don't do that to me, kid. I'm not in the mood to be tantalized."

"OK. All that bullshit about Jason being emotionally disturbed was for setting up the boy for a plea of insanity. You and I know he is an insufferable jerk, but he's still his mother's favorite, and she wants to protect him. On the other hand, she wants to pin Rutledge's murder on him . . . to protect somebody else."

"Sounds plausible. Go on."

"Who's the somebody else? Lisa? From what I know, she and her mother aren't very friendly. Farnham? Could be. But I think Farnham's too smart. He injured people for a living. He didn't kill 'em. Well, *many* of 'em."

"Who does that leave, besides me and you? *Somebody* killed Rutledge, execution style. Who's left?"

"What's the guy's name? The big stud I saw going into the house in Glendale."

"Oh, yeah. Eddie Colucci. Former hit man. Partner of Rutledge in the Vegas place. Aw, shit, he's too obvious. He'd never turn out to be the killer on 'Murder, She Wrote.' "

"This is not fiction, Riordan. We are dealing with a real murder here. This is like cop work. The most suspicious character is often the guy who did the deed."

"Tell you what, lady. You stay here with me and just *think* a while. Then, a little later, you can fix me some dinner. Afterwards we'll watch Monday Night Football, and see some *real* sport."

"I'll fix you something to eat, but I'm not going to watch your damn' football game."

We sat around in silence, both wrapped in deep thought for the rest of the afternoon. That is, *she* was wrapped in deep thought. I was only faking it. I didn't want to think.

Later she ran down to Bruno's for something to eat, and came puffing up the hill clutching a barbecued chicken and a bag of pretzels.

"The pretzels are for your football game. Let's eat the chicken now. It's still hot."

I don't remember how the chicken tasted, nor do I recall just who played in that football game. The whole evening is a kind of blur now.

But I *do* remember the next day. I'll never forget the next day.

The next day was October 17.

24

The greasy ribs flew in all directions.

I DO NOT remember who played whom on Monday Night Football on the night of October 16, 1989. I *do* remember that Al Michaels wasn't there because he was in San Francisco to broadcast the World Series. It's strange that I should forget all the details of a football game. It's the only sport I was ever any good at. I guess it's because it's one game that doesn't require you to hit a ball with some kind of instrument. Never could do that. And don't ask me how I could miss with a tennis racquet.

Let's see, now. Reiko went home right after we had the chicken. I sat down a little later with my pretzels and a can of 7-Up to watch the game. Monday Night Football starts at 6:00 P.M. on the West Coast, you know. Makes it pretty convenient. Most of the games run until after midnight in the East.

I watched the game, finished the pretzels, and went to bed. I was feeling a little better. The pain in my shoulder and arm had diminished a good deal, and I had a hard time resisting the urge to remove the wrappings that immobilized my right arm. Anyhow, I struggled into my night clothes, and went to bed, exhausted from my activities of the day.

Next morning I was awakened by the telephone, ringing insistently downstairs. I had forgotten to take it to the bedroom with me and I stumbled down the stairs, freezing my ass in my nightshirt.

I snarled into the phone: "What!"

"It's Reiko. And don't get nasty. I just talked to my cousin Sab in Glendale. He tells me that the Rutledge house has been under police surveillance for a couple of months and that I was observed checking out the mail. Of all the nerve!"

"You called me just to tell me that? What are you, crazy?"

"Aren't you going to ask me why the place was being staked out by the cops?"

"Why was the place being staked out by the cops?"

"Well, it seems that Rutledge was suspected of conducting a high-level drug operation from the house in Glendale. The police were checking on everybody who arrived or left. Sab says they knew all about the man's connections in Las Vegas, but this was something new. They got an anonymous tip. . . ."

"*What!* The cops using man-hours on an anonymous tip? That's absurd."

"Not really. The guy who phoned in the tip seemed to know a lot about Rutledge and his operation. Sab says they just had to check it out."

"What else?"

"It seems that the surveillance had been going on for about three weeks. During the first week, Farnham had been seen going in and out several times."

"How'd they know it was Farnham?"

"They didn't. Sab just described him. White hair, black clothes. Couldn't have been anybody else. Another visitor must have been Colucci. And get this: Jason Andrews was hanging around. He wasn't in New Jersey going to school, at least during the past three weeks."

"How about Stephanie?"

"Oh, she was around and about. And so was your friend, or should I say 'amigo', Angel Garcia. But both of them seemed to be commuting to and from the Burbank Airport. The cops trailed them a couple of times."

"Is that all? It doesn't tell me much that I didn't already know. Except about Jason. I was under the impression that he just flew in from Princeton."

"All I know is what the Glendale police know. Sab promised that he'd call me if anything else turned up."

I suddenly felt weary, and became aware that my feet, warm and perspiring from the bed, were forming a film of ice on the tile floor. My teeth began to chatter. I said: "Talk to you later, Reiko-san." Slowly I climbed the stairs and went back to bed.

When I came to again, it was eleven o'clock by the digital thing-a-ma-jig on the desk opposite the bed. I have to believe it's somewhere near right because I don't know how to set it. Every time the power goes out I call Sally, and she comes over and re-adjusts the thing to the proper hour and minute.

It was still chilly in the upstairs bedroom. There's no heat up there except what creeps up the stairs from the old floor furnace. It's like original equipment for a lot of the old houses in Carmel. You're supposed to use the fireplace downstairs, or buy an electric heater for the bedroom. I just hadn't got around to it yet. The heater, I mean. It doesn't get all that cold ever in Carmel. We have frost now and then, but that's something else I call Sally for. She always keeps me warm. And she smells a hell of a lot better than the furnace *or* the old fireplace.

I went down to fix breakfast. Sally had left a carton of orange juice in the refrigerator, and I knew how to boil water from my instant coffee. To be honest, I've grown used to the stuff and I kind of like it. And it's easier than going through all that ritual of making real coffee. I had pulled on an old robe and much older slippers and was wondering what to do next, when I heard a key in the door. Sally came in with a bag of cinnamon-raisin bagels.

"It's nearer lunch time than breakfast, but I knew you'd sleep late. Here. They're still warm, and there's some cream cheese in that little plastic cup."

"Stick around, Sal. I'm getting my strength back."

"I've got work to do. How do you think I can pay my bills if I don't keep working?"

"Just don't pay 'em. Or do like I do: Put 'em all in a drawer and draw out one or two a month blindfolded. Keeps all your creditors off balance."

"Goodbye, Riordan." She kissed me gently but firmly, and went on her way.

The rest of that day dragged on. I tried watching some of the TV shows I'd got used to in the hospital. It didn't seem the same. I picked up a book I'd been meaning to read by a guy who claimed that all he ever needed to know he learned in kindergarten. It was wonderful. I read on and on until nearly four o'clock.

Then I remembered that the World Series broadcast would come on at five. As I've said, I'm really no baseball fan. But this Series involved the Giants and the Oakland A's. I mean, as an old San Franciscan, I would have been banished forever from the Washington Square Bar and Grill if I had failed to take an interest in the Series of '89.

Since it appeared that nobody was going to bring me dinner, I called down to Bruno's for something to eat. Their truck is always at the ready, and since I am only a couple of blocks away, they indulge me sometimes.

About five o'clock, I sat down in front of the TV with a plate of ribs on my lap, and a loaf of sour French bread on the little table beside me. I had turned on the machine and Al Michaels was just opening his spiel preliminary to the baseball game. I munched contentedly on my ribs and bread, fully aware that nothing I was eating would contribute to my longevity, when it seemed like a huge dog seized my house by the chimney and was shaking the hell out of it.

The greasy ribs flew in all directions. The plate skidded off my lap and made a bee line for the fireplace where it shattered. I got up and staggered towards the archway into the kitchen out of some instinct that told me that you're supposed to stand in doorways during an earthquake. I clutched the wall near the arch and held on for dear life.

I would have sworn that that monster shake went on for a minute and a half. Now, as everybody knows, the earth trembled for a mere fifteen seconds. But you never think of that during a quake. I've felt a lot of 'em in my time, and they usually last only long enough to let you know what's happening. Then they stop. And there's that feeling. Whew! That was quite a jolt. And you go on doing what you were doing.

But this time, the shaking didn't seem to want to stop. Then that *other* feeling comes over you. Is this the "Big One"? I remember distinctly asking myself that question.

And then it stopped. The lights had gone out, and I hadn't noticed. The TV, of course, was dead. I picked up the phone and *it* was dead. Outside it was deathly quiet. Instinctively, I dashed out the front door to see if any other human being was left on earth.

A man appeared from a house across the street. "Didja feel that?" he shouted. Unnecessary question of the day. "Yeah, that was some shake", was the best I could do. I walked around the house to check for damage in the fading light. We were still on Daylight Saving Time and night had not yet fallen in California.

I went back in the house. In about fifteen minutes, another tremor shook the house. An "aftershock", that's what they call 'em. I stopped to see if anything was going to fall off the shelves or if the ceiling was going to fall on *me*. Nothing happened.

Better get candles, I thought. Where's the goddam flashlight? No battery operated radio. What the hell.

I found the flashlight, rustled up a few candles and, in a moment of brilliant inspiration, went out and turned on the radio in the car.

For two hours I listened to reports from San Francisco. There had been a lot of damage. A double-deck freeway had collapsed. Part of the Bay Bridge had caved in. It was the worst quake since 1906. I listened until I started worrying about the battery in the car, decided I couldn't do anything constructive in the dark. So I went back into the house, flopped down on the couch so I could be reasonably near the door, and went to sleep.

I didn't dream that the earthquake would help me solve the Rutledge-Farnham case. But it did.

25

"Did you feel it much?"

I AWOKE IN A state of confusion in the strong light of day. As consciousness returned slowly, the events of the night came back. I looked around the room.

The candle I had left burning on the mantel had used up all of its wax, which had produced a colorful cascade down the valuable antique stone of the fireplace. I was lucky it hadn't keeled over and started a fire. Nothing seemed to be out of place, although the pictures on the walls were all askew. I left 'em that way for days.

In the kitchen I was astounded to see that all of the glassware had remained on the shelf. Not one broken plate or cup. I checked the pilot burners on the stove, and sniffed around for gas leaks.

Warily, I climbed the stairs. In the bedroom, some books had fallen out of a small case near the bed. A spare roll of toilet paper had been shaken off the john. It had unrolled itself neatly across the bathroom floor and out into the hall.

Downstairs again, I stupidly snapped on the television. Nothing. Power still out. I remembered hearing on the radio that the Moss Landing power plant had gone down. Pacific Gas & Electric serves most of Monterey County from Moss Landing. For an hour or two I went around flipping light switches as usual but in vain. God, what creatures of habit we are.

I sat down on the couch and stared at the wall. It is discomforting to be alone in the world. I longed for the hum and rattle of the noisy refrigerator. Then it occurred to me that all of the frozen Snickers bars would thaw. And the milk would sour. And the orange juice would get warm.

All of us in California have been warned over and over again to prepare for a big shocker. Get in bottled water, lay in a supply of canned goods. Get a camp stove. Get emergency lights and plenty of batteries.

Batteries! Maybe they'd have batteries down at Bruno's. I raced up the stairs. That is, I raced faster than I had been able to since I was shot. Flinging caution to the winds, I peeled off the wrappings on my right arm and tried to straighten it out. Try as I might, I couldn't get it straight. The wound was heavily bandaged and wide strips of adhesive tape covered part of my chest and all of my right shoulder blade. I remembered that the nurse said to go to my personal physician in a week to have the bandage removed and the wound redressed. I also remembered that I *have* no personal physician. I have this feeling that the physicians are the guys who are kicking up the prices of Carmel real estate. They buy the $600K houses and let 'em sit there as write-offs. These places are great for getting away from patients on the weekends. Sick people are a drag, anyhow.

Miracle of miracles, I got into a running suit with a hood, pulled on a mismatched pair of sweat socks and a pair of worn sneakers.

Into the chill of the October morning I strode, feeling like a true survivor. I stopped long enough to take another check of the house. The sixty-one-year-old stone chimney was intact. There appeared to be no cracks in the foundation.

Down the steep hill to Junipero Street where a long line of chatty people stretched out from the front door of Bruno's.

Everybody seemed so goddam cheerful. A ten-year-old in line ahead of me proudly told of being at Candlestick Park the night before, during the earthquake. A young couple was eager to tell all about coming over Highway 17 when it began to bounce around. They arrived at the bottom of the hill, on the ocean side of the Santa Cruz mountains safely, and came on down to a darkened motel. There were no restaurants open and they hadn't had anything to eat, but they were happy. God, were they happy! They were young, and it was a long night.

When I made it into the store they were out of batteries. I knew they would be out of batteries. I meandered around and picked up a couple of cans of soup and a box of saltines. At least the gas was still on at the house.

Pumping back up the hill took a lot out of me. It's usually a challenge to us older folks, but that day it was damn' near impossible. As I neared the driveway, I looked at my cherished Mercedes. I couldn't remember when it was brought home, although I sat in it during the night listening to the radio. For the first time I saw the broken rear window and the smashed glove compartment. Hurt me worse than any earthquake.

The phone was ringing when I got in the door. The phone! The outside world! Somebody I know is still out there somewhere!

"H'lo," I gasped.

"Are you all right?" Sally's voice blasted into my ear, causing me to jerk the receiver away. "Pat? Are you there? Are you hurt?"

"I am *here*. I am aching and out of breath. The phone wasn't working, so I walked down to the store. I'm weak. But all in one piece. How are *you?*"

"Shook up. Just shook up. Power's out still. Did you feel it much?"

"Sal, that is a dumb, unnecessary question. Of course I felt it. It shook the livin' hell out of the house. But as far as I can tell, there's nothing much damaged. Except, maybe, my nervous system. I hear a lot of people got killed in Oakland."

"Yes, and isn't it terrible about the bridge? We didn't get it as much out here in the Valley, I guess. But I was scared. Boy, was I scared!"

"What are you going to do, Sally? Coming in to the office? If you do will you bring me some batteries."

"I've got no batteries. And Safeway is closed out here." Sally lives in a condo in Carmel Valley, about half way to the Village.

"Well, stop by if you decide to come in. You better check that upstairs office of yours. You never know."

"Keep in touch, Pat. I . . . I love you."

"OK. Marry me."

"Nope. Maybe later." And she hung up.

That's the way it goes with Sally and me. I keep proposing to her, and she keeps turning me down.

I stumbled around the house wondering what to do next. I picked up the books. I kept turning the gas burners on the stove off and on, to make sure they'd work. I called the power company and a guy told me that if I didn't smell gas, *not* to turn off the outside gas valve. He sounded harried.

The unmistakable sound of Reiko's Honda came from outside. I looked out as she pulled up alongside the Mercedes.

She got out of the car and opened the hatch. From it she extracted a huge bag of groceries which she brought into the house without even saying "hello." Abruptly, she turned and went back to the car to fetch an equally large box which, I later learned, contained all those things that the earthquake preparedness people had been insisting that we get.

"*There,*" she said. "I knew you wouldn't have any of this stuff, so I went out and got it for you. You owe me"—she checked a small pad which she plucked from her purse—"fifty-six dollars and thirty cents. And a couple of gallons of gas."

"How did you do that? Where did you get all that stuff?"

"My Uncle Shiro—our landlord, remember?—can get anything, any time. His best friend runs a grocery store in Seaside. And one of our relatives, I forget which, has a sporting good store in Monterey. I got all the camp stuff wholesale."

"Reiko-san, are you all right? Did anything happen to your apartment."

"I was at my aerobics class when the thing hit. We didn't notice much. Except that when we bounced, the floor seemed to bounce back. As a matter of fact, we didn't notice *anything* until the power went out and the music stopped. The apartment is OK, I guess. Nothing broken, as far as I could tell."

"Are you going to ask me how I am. I was here all by myself, wounded, you know." I tried to look hurt.

"Shit, Riordan, I knew *you'd* be all right. This old house is solid. And did you know that the entire Monterey Peninsula is one block of granite? Over in Watsonville, though, they really got it bad. Soft soil over there. Alluvial soil, fertile soil."

"What are you going to do now?"

"Goin' to the office. I *don't* think there could be any damage, but I'll have to see. I'm not sure what this power thing is going to do to my computer. I'd better unplug it until they turn on the juice. Sometimes there's a surge and it can really blow the guts out of a computer."

"Let me know, will you, if there's any damage. And see if there are any messages . . . " I stopped. The message machine wouldn't work, either. We are so goddam dependent on electricity.

"Yeah, I thought about that. Probably if there were any messages on it, they got wiped. Or maybe they didn't. I don't know how those things work. They say we'll get the power back in maybe seventy-two hours."

"Oh, God," I groaned. "My radio won't work. My refrigerator will cook my Snickers bars."

Reiko pushed the bag of groceries at me. "There's plenty of stuff here that doesn't need refrigeration. You'll be all right. I'll keep in touch. OK?"

I nodded and smiled a brave little smile. "See you later, kid. Take care."

At that moment, another aftershock hit us. For about four seconds we just stared at each other. Then Reiko said, "So long, sport. I'll call you."

She was out the back door and off up Sixth to Carpenter and thence to Monterey. I waved, but she never looked back.

26

"Gee, Pat, speak of the devil."

SHE DIDN'T bring me any batteries. But maybe nobody *had* any batteries. But I didn't have a portable radio anyhow. So why was I so irritated?

Sometimes Reiko accuses me of what the Japanese call *enryo*. There's no English equivalent. The word just describes a feeling of reluctance to ask for something when you really want it. Like, gee, I don't want you to go to any trouble. I would never have asked her to bring me all the groceries and equipment, even though I needed help badly. Funny, I never have that trouble with Sally. But then she seldom does what I ask her to do anyhow.

Everybody in the country knows about the Earthquake of '89, and its aftermath. I'm not going into detail about it here. It was a mean one, and even though a lot of us have been through shakes of various intensities, nobody alive has felt anything like this. Oh, there are some folks still around who were kids in 1906, but it's likely that their memories are mostly what their parents told them. *And* what they have embroidered onto the bare facts. That's what myths are made of. Every teller of tales adds a little something down the line.

The earthquake *is* important to this story, though, because in an oblique sort of way it led me to the answer to a very important question. Which gave me all the information I needed to pin down the shooter who got me and the murderer of Harrison Rutledge.

But it didn't happen right away. I mean, the day after and for several more days, nothing much got done by me or anyone else. The electricity was restored piecemeal to the Peninsula, from north to south, and the lights went on in Carmel about twenty-four hours after they had gone out. By that time I had accumulated nine candles, and had arranged them neatly on the mantel, waiting for nightfall. They're still there.

I remember wandering around town, looking for signs of damage. There really wasn't any. I watched a lot of TV, spellbound by the often-repeated shots of the fallen freeway, the gap in the bridge, the old houses in Watsonville, tilted at crazy angles. Probably nobody in Northern California has watched that much TV since the assassination of John Kennedy in 1963. I know I haven't.

But life goes on. I hadn't forgotten about Eric Farnham or Stephanie Rutledge. And disturbing images of the Andrews siblings remained in the back of my mind. I was involved up to my navel in a murder case. But it took a little while for my enthusiasm for investigation to return.

On the third day, which must have been the 20th, I made up my mind to return to action. I had finished all the soup Reiko and I had bought. Sally had come over and made dinner Wednesday, and we went down to Casanova on Thursday. Normality had just about returned to the Peninsula.

Reiko and I had talked several times on the phone. My arm was straightening out. Thursday morning I went down to a local drop-in medical office and had my bandage changed. The doctor said I was healing nicely and charged me $60. I immediately forgot his name.

Friday, Balestreri called. "Did you enjoy the entertainment the other night, Patrick? We thought that since you were laid up and probably bored, we'd stage a little shimmy-show for you. Did you applaud?"

"Lay off or I'll have your badge. My cousin is a county supervisor. I lived through it. So did everybody else I know. Now, what's your question?"

He got serious. "It is time for us to get together on this Farnham thing, pal. From what I have been able to put together, your client is the most probable suspect in the murder of Harrison Rutledge. We've been in touch with the Glendale police, and it seems that Farnham had been carrying on with Mrs. Rutledge. Pretty good motive, don't you think?"

" 'Carrying on'? My God, Tony, nobody says that anymore. Where've you been? The current euphemisms are 'sleeping with' or 'having sex'. I've never understood that last one, though. Doesn't everybody have sex? I mean, you've got one sex and your wife has another, right? 'Carrying on'. Come off it. There's a very useful four-letter word which, in its many forms, may be used as a noun, a verb, an adjective, or. . . ."

I was stalling, trying to think of a way to dodge the issue of having to turn Farnham in. It wasn't that I wouldn't have turned him in, but rather that I didn't know where he *was.*

"Get serious," he said. "You've got to hand Farnham over to us. And soon. I've played your game, now you play mine. You've got twenty-four hours to turn him in. And that's stretching it a whole hell of a lot."

Tony's call started the creative juices flowing. I knew I had to do *something*. I just didn't know what I had to do.

Call Reiko. I had to think very hard to remember my own office number.

Her voice came over like warm honey: "Riordan and Masuda. Can we help you?"

"Has Farnham called? In the last couple of days? What do you hear from your cousin at the Glendale cop house? Anything from Garcia? Has either of those cretinous Andrews kids shown up?"

"Hold it, sport. I will try to answer your questions in the order received. No. Nothing. Nothing. Neither. Does that help?"

"Well, what the hell have you been doing down there while I suffer here, a helpless invalid?"

"I've been straightening up the files, paying current bills . . . and making money. I've accepted two assignments from attorneys and a juicy divorce case from a friend of George Spelvin. You can help if you get off your ass in a couple of days. You really don't need your right arm."

"Reiko, Balestreri called. He's pressing me to turn Farnham in to him. I've got to find Farnham. But I can't let him know the sheriff is after him. Any ideas?"

"There's really nothing I can do. . . ." There was a long pause.

"Gee, Pat, speak of the devil. The guy just walked in. Shall I have him wait?"

The mysterious Mr. Farnham. Evil incarnate? Or just another scofflaw trying to make a dishonest buck. Tune in tomorrow. . . .

"Put him on," I said. "You're sure it's him, now. White hair, black clothes? Reeboks?"

"Mr. Riordan wants to talk with you, Mr. Farnham." I could hear the sweet smile in her voice.

"Farnham here, Riordan. Anything you want to tell me? Any tidbit of information? Are you earning your money? Or should I politely request a refund?" The accent was more noticeable on the phone. Just a little *too* Oxford.

"You know where I live, Eric. Why don't you come over to Carmel. We could talk. It's comfortable here. Warm and comfortable. We could sit on nice soft chairs . . . and talk. I presume you're driving."

"I bought a motorcycle. I accept your invitation. Be there in a jif. Cheer-o."

I guess he handed the phone back to Reiko. There was a small silence, and then: "He's gone, Pat. What did you say to him?"

"I invited him to tea, small one. Did you get the crack about politely requesting a refund? You know about Farnham's 'requests', don't you? You don't give him what he asks for, he breaks your legs. Look, do me a favor. Call Balestreri. Tell him that Farnham is on his way over here. If he wants the man, he can have him. Tell him to look for a motorcycle. If it's here, he can come on in. If it isn't, he's to wait 'til Farnham arrives. If he's too late, bring paramedics."

"Why don't you call him yourself? Farnham's not going to get there in five minutes."

"My hands are sweating. Besides, you come over on the phone better than I do. I. . . ."

"Hang up."

"OK."

27

"Well, what do you have to say for yourself, old boy?"

I SAT BACK quietly in my only easy chair to await the coming of the white-haired menace and tried to figure out why I had done what I did. Inviting Farnham to my house for a *tête-à-tête* no longer seemed like a smart idea. What if Reiko couldn't get through to Balestreri? Would she call the Carmel police? In this mile-square town there's always a police cruiser only minutes away. Sure, Reiko's no dumbbell. She'd call somebody. Any sheriff's deputy would do, although I really didn't know the other guys that well, and Tony Balestreri was the only one who cared anything about me. Aw hell, Reiko would do the right thing.

Farnham could get from my office on Alvarado Street in Monterey to my house at Sixth and Santa Rita in Carmel in about twenty minutes, given good traffic conditions. Maybe faster on a motorcycle. Oh, yeah, a good deal faster on a motorcycle. I listened for one, but the sound of traffic on Ocean Avenue a short block away was all I could hear.

Maybe Greg Farrell has been right all along. I should have a gun. No, I *shouldn't* have a gun. If I had a gun, I'd probably kill myself. *Not* on purpose, you understand, but as the result of, say, dropping it butt-first on the tile floor and leaning over to pick it up when it went off. I saw a guy do that one time, a replacement second lieutenant in Korea. Damnedest thing I ever witnessed. The piece hit the floor and the slug got the man right between the eyes.

I got up and paced the living room. It's about 24½ feet long, incidentally, and 11 feet wide. I looked around at the crooked pictures and made a mental note to straighten them. I walked over to the thermostat and turned the heat up precisely five degrees. The floor furnace by the front door came on with a whoomp.

Nervously, I ran up the stairs and peered out the window at the landing. Two very old ladies were making their way up the hill, clinging to each other and to bags of groceries. Nice clean arteries there. Pump up Sixth Avenue every day and you won't accumulate the crap that clogs the bloodstream. Those girls are closing in on eighty, and they'll probably live to be a hundred, easy.

After about ten minutes, I could make out the slow approach up Santa Rita from the north of just the front end of a white automobile. It stopped. All I could see was the hood and one headlight. I hoped it was one of those beautiful sedans with the green stripe that Sheriff's deputies drive around. Maybe my life would be spared, after all.

Let me assure you that I am not a wimp. As a foot-soldier, I never disobeyed an order, never shrank from a challenge. In my younger days, I would never go out of my way to avoid a fight. I wouldn't *start* a fight, but I'm proud to say that oftener than not, I got in the last punch. When Helen, my one and only wife, was killed, I got into bar brawls altogether too frequently, and my name is on police blotters in a number of communities.

But in my mid-fifties (slipping into the *latter* fifties), I figure that I cannot take too many chances. I've made it this far, and I'm a little reluctant to let go of what has been an interesting and fairly satisfying life.

My right shoulder was beginning to ache. Jesus, I thought, even if I *had* a gun, I couldn't handle it. There's not much I can do with my left hand. I sure as hell can't shoot with it. I was a terrible shot with a hand gun anyhow, having failed to qualify with a GI .45 by hitting almost everything on the pistol range but the target.

At that moment of frightening introspection, I heard the motorcycle. It was unmistakable, the vroom-vroom of the cycle coming to a stop under my window. I looked out from the upstairs landing to see

Eric Farnham remove his helmet and leather gloves, stow them in a carrier on the back of his machine, and come to my kitchen door.

I slowly descended the staircase. The handrail is on the right coming down, and I couldn't use it to steady myself with my bum arm. Farnham was banging on the door with his fist. I didn't want to fall down the steps and fracture my skull before he had a chance to fracture it. No, that's wrong, isn't it? Somebody's got to get in here and apprehend the man *before* he fractures my skull.

Farnham kept hitting my kitchen door with what sounded like a blunt instrument. I reached the bottom of the stairs and strode through the living room and kitchen to the door.

"Don't break it down, Eric," I yelled, "it's irreplaceable. They don't make 'em like that anymore."

He stood there on the tree round that serves as my back step and smiled his oily smile. "Good to see you again, old boy. How's the shoulder? Wound's healing well, I hope."

"Come on in." His eyes darted around suspiciously as he entered. Obviously, Farnham didn't trust me. No reason why he should.

We went into the living room. I slumped down on the couch while Farnham took a straight chair near the front door.

"Well, what do you have to say for yourself, old boy? Any cheerful news to impart?" The man was smiling, but there was a threatening glint in his eyes.

"Eric, I sort of have a feeling that you and Harrison Rutledge knew each other. As a matter of fact, I think that Rutledge bought Felicia Montalvo's house on your recommendation. And I think you had a pretty good motive for killing him."

Farnham's expression didn't change. "You're on pretty dangerous ground, old boy. I come here to consult with you as a client, and you try to pin a murder rap on me. That's not very nice, you know."

I noticed that the white-haired man's hands had curled into fists, but he was still smiling that wicked smile.

"Are you going to fire me, Eric? I still have no earthly idea where Felicia's money is. But I'm picking up a lot of other knowledge."

The smile slowly vanished. "I might kill you, Riordan. I didn't shoot you. If I had shot at you, I would have killed you. I didn't kill Rutledge. Somebody tried to make it look like a professional job, but it wasn't my job. Oh, I've killed men. And I'm very good at it. A lot of people I've just crippled, but I've killed a few. But you really couldn't call it murder. Just business. I *might* kill you. But I won't. I'm not guilty of any provable crime at the moment. And, besides, I just saw that clumsy deputy friend of yours, the one with the mustache, passing by the window. He should be at the door now. By all means, let him in."

Tony stood there staring at me when I opened the front door. Farnham looked up at him from his chair and smiled. "Hello, there, Sergeant. It's pleasant to see you again. How've you been?"

28

He was such an evil sonofabitch.

BALESTRERI WAS confused and disbelieving, but he hauled the smiling and cooperative Farnham off anyhow on a charge of suspicion of homicide. There wasn't much else he could do. I think he had expected something approaching a shoot-out, with the snarling criminal backed into a corner threatening to blast the both of us.

Farnham, though, had cheerfully extended his wrists to be cuffed and waited patiently while Balestreri went back to the car to look for his manacles, which he'd left in the glove compartment. The white-haired man chatted pleasantly about the unnaturally warm weather and the recent earthquake.

"I'm surprised, Riordan. I thought this old house of yours would fall down. I was in a room on the top floor of a motel down on Junipero Street. Place rocked like one of those abominable rides at Disneyland. Thought it was all over. I had always thought that imminent death would cause my past life to pass before me, but there wasn't time, do you see? Not time enough to think of a blasted thing."

I couldn't imagine Farnham on a ride at Disneyland. The idea set my mind racing. What the hell had a self-confessed killer and enforcer been doing at Disneyland? Following a victim? Planning to do the blighter in at Space Mountain? Push him out of one of those flying centrifuge things so the body would sail over Fantasyland and be impaled on a minaret? I didn't ask him.

After the deputy and his prisoner had gone I made myself a cup of coffee and sat down. My adrenalin had been pumping and my pulse needed time to settle.

It was not easy to admit to myself, but Farnham was probably innocent of shooting me and murdering Harrison Rutledge. He was such an evil sonofabitch. One likes to think that patently evil people commit all the heinous crimes in the universe. But the truth is that many murders are committed by the best friends or spouses of the victims. The act of murder is most often an act of passion. Farnham had admitted murdering for a fee. But he and his ilk are relatively few. The bullet-riddled body of the gang leader in a deserted alley, or photographed clutching a bloody checkered table cloth in an Italian restaurant—these things make the front page. But this is business, only business. The gregarious, middle-class woman found bludgeoned to death on her front lawn does not get her picture on the front page of the newspaper. But it's safe to say that whoever killed her knew her very well.

So it was fairly easy to believe that Farnham, the business man, wouldn't kill except for profit. On the other hand, it was hard to imagine that he could realize any profit in killing Rutledge. Revenge? Out of the question. Eric Farnham wouldn't risk his neck for simple revenge. Love? The white-haired man, I am sure, is totally incapable of love. He's probably had as many women in as many positions as the human mind can conceive. But I'm sure he never experienced post-coital guilt or sadness. To dredge up an old expression I learned in the Army, "Wham, bam, thank you ma'am." Only I doubt that Eric ever thanked anybody for anything.

When my heartbeat had returned to normal and my breathing came more easily, I decided to take a walk for some exercise. My right shoulder was throbbing a bit, so I took a couple of aspirins, pulled on a sweater, clapped an ancient, shapeless hat on my head, and went out.

It was a chilly day. The wind was coming up, a fresh breeze off the sea, and high clouds were scudding across the sky. I turned up the collar of my baggy coat sweater, and buried my chin in my chest. It felt like rain, although the sun was shining. The clouds made mere blips in the sunlight. I felt the pull in my calves as I plunged up the hill on Sixth Avenue.

As I neared the intersection of Sixth Avenue and Carpenter Street, I heard the sound of a high-powered engine behind me. Ordinarily, I would pay no attention to that kind of noise. People make a habit of starting down at Torres and putting the accelerator pedal on the floor up the hill. But on this occasion something told me to look back.

Coming at me at high speed was a massive pickup truck, with springs and tires that lifted the driver's head ten feet off the road. All I could see of the driver in the instant that I looked back was a hard hat and dark glasses. The truck was bearing down on me with the firm purpose of running me down.

My reflexes work pretty well for an old soldier. By some miracle of instinct and fear of death, I catapulted myself sideways into the vacant lot at the southwest corner of Sixth and Carpenter. The driver of the truck tried to come after me, but hit the formidable stump of a live oak and gave up the chase. The truck went into reverse, noisily dug out of the lot backwards and, with much sound and fury, skidded around the corner going north on Carpenter, narrowly missing a County Transit bus coming up from Ocean.

I lay on my back in the leaves and brush for a long moment. A woman came out of the house across the street, looked around, didn't see me, shook her head wearily, and went back inside. I got up shakily and pulled at the stuff sticking to my sweater.

There wasn't any doubt in my mind now. It had to have been the same truck. The driver must have been the one who shot me. And *this time* I was certain. This guy was trying to kill me.

29

"Somebody tried to kill you again?"

IT IS VERY HARD to explain, but I felt a sort of exultation as I walked back down Sixth Avenue to the house. Happy as hell that I was still alive, of course, but something else, too. It was clear now. There *was* somebody trying to kill me. *Or* there were two or more people involved, one of whom was a rotten shot.

There was still the little matter of the bullet fired into the empty bed at the hospital. Even a rotten shot wouldn't fire at the wrong damn target. Unless . . .

It had to be more than one person. Person A had tried to kill me at the intersection of Pacific and Soledad in Monterey, and again just now on Sixth Avenue in Carmel. Person B fired the shot at the hospital mainly to scare me off so I *wouldn't* get killed.

And I had a dandy assortment of suspects: a beautiful woman in late middle age; a skinny, petulant youth with a nasty temper; a young woman who dressed in leather with a bare belly button; and a large Latino detective from Los Angeles who was probably no better than he had to be.

So it was with hope in my heart that I trotted—even skipped—down the hill after almost being flattened by a large pickup truck. Downhill I can trot. Uphill, forget it.

As I neared the house, I noticed that I was accompanied by a large shaggy dog of indeterminate age and breed. He—or, as I learned later in the usual fashion—*she* had seen me leap into the vacant lot and perhaps felt that she could do something for me. I slowed to a walk, and reached down to scratch her behind the ears. She looked up at me with liquid eyes and a doggy smile. With an air of authority, she escorted me to the front door and calmly lay down on my deck.

The phone was ringing as I went through the door. I walked slowly across the tiles to answer it, feeling pretty self-satisfied and devil-may-care.

"Riordan," I said, trying to sound as world-weary as I could.

"Your phone has rung fourteen times. I was just about to hang up. Where the hell have you been?" It was Reiko, sounding only mildly exasperated. She couldn't really bear down on an invalid, could she?

"I was taking a constitutional, Reiko-san. Up the hill, down the hill. Good for the heart and the lungs, for clearing the arteries, for. . . ."

"Stephanie Rutledge called. She wants to see you. She wouldn't tell me anything, but she sounded pretty desperate. Not like the super-cool lady we saw the other day."

"Well, I think I can drive now." I wasn't at all sure of that. My right arm was still a little crooked, and I winced at the thought of my little car with all of the damage. "I'll just run out to the Point and see the lady. Who knows? She might be ready to confess to something. By the way, somebody just tried to run me down in a pickup truck. Our illustrious landlord, your Uncle Shiro operates a gardening service. Do you suppose he's trying to get rid of me?"

"Come again, Riordan. Somebody tried to kill you again? You're kidding. You got to be kidding."

"No, seriously, my dear friend. This time there was no doubt about it. The driver drew a bead on me and was bent on leaving tread marks on my head. Only my lightning reflexes saved me."

There was a pause at the other end. "This is getting scary. When you got shot, I thought it must be some kind of accident. You know, a warning bullet that got closer than it should have. It was just a flesh wound, you know."

I grew indignant. "Flesh wound or not, dearie, it was very painful and dangerously near fatal. How could you dismiss my misery in such a cavalier manner?" I was needling her, and she knew it.

"You know what I mean. We've both been working on the notion that all these attacks on you have been part of a scheme to get you off this case. *Now,* though, it looks like somebody really means business. Watch your step, Riordan. Hey, maybe it's Mrs. Rutledge."

"How could it be Mrs. Rutledge, sweetie, when Mrs. Rutledge was just trying to get me at the office. How long ago did she call?"

"Minutes. Plus, of course, the time it took for you to answer your phone. Fourteen rings. . . ."

"See? It couldn't have been the fair Stephanie. So. She wants me to come out to the house, eh? Probably try to seduce me, you know. She has a weakness for truly virile men. *You* told me that. And who is more virile than I?"

"Would you believe Pee-wee Herman? Look, if you go out there, be careful. Stephanie might not be dangerous, but the character with the truck might be hanging around. And if you take another bullet and survive, you'll be hell to live with."

"I'll take that as an expression of deep affection, Reiko-san. One thing you can do for me, though."

"What?"

"Call anybody you know who can run a trace on a modified pickup truck, black or dark blue, oversized tires, white California license plate, partial number. . . ."

"Wait a minute. Let me get a pencil. Say, how did you manage to get a license number with that thing bearing down on you?"

"Got it on the fly, pal. As the truck skidded around the corner onto Carpenter. Couldn't catch it all, but what I got should help." I gave her what I could remember.

"I'll call my Uncle Tony Umemoto. He's a lieutenant on the Pacific Grove police."

"How come I never heard you mention him?"

"We've never had any business out of Pacific Grove, dummny. It's a peaceful community. I live there."

There is so much of the Mysterious East about Reiko. Whenever I feel that I am at a dead end in a case, she turns up another relative who can resolve my problem. Maybe I should turn the business over to her, and become the world's worst travel agent under the supervision of Sally Morse.

"Riordan, are you still there? You must be, because I didn't hear you hang up. I just thought of something. Do you think you should go out to the Point unarmed? You don't even have your blackthorn stick at home, do you? Do you have anything around the house that you could use to protect yourself? Like a meat cleaver, or something?"

That made me smile. "Small one, I have managed to pile up a substantial number of years without carrying a weapon. Except, of course, in the Forgotten War." It's a goddam shame about that business in Korea. There's no monument. There's very damn' little literature. And a lot of young men died.

"Suit yourself. But don't say I didn't warn you." There was silence, and then an afterthought. Then a very small voice, almost a whisper: "I don't want to lose you."

"Bye-bye," I said, and hung up.

30

A certain melvolence, masked by that persistent smile.

I WAS STRUCK by a brief fit of melancholy when I got in my little rusting, oxidized, battered Mercedes. The bullet hole in the rear window let in a lot of cold air. The smashed lid of the glove compartment looked forlorn and permanently maimed. I've never heard of a body shop that works on damaged glove compartments. The fact is that I have always been just a little bit ashamed to have bought a luxury automobile with my late wife's insurance money. I've tried to tell myself that Helen would have wanted it that way. But that doesn't work too well. She had paid all the premiums on a hundred thousand dollar insurance policy which doubled for accidental death. And then she was killed by a drunk on the 280 freeway.

It took me about a year and a half to go through $200,000 tax-free. The car is all I have left. I really don't know what happened to the rest of the money. I dimly remember that I bought lots and lots of rounds of drinks. When Reiko happened upon me in a drunken stupor in my San Francisco office, some divine providence must have been in operation. She *said* she was looking for work, but she must have been sent from heaven. When I offered her far less than she was worth, she took it, probably because I represented a challenge. She got me sober and productive, and asked little in return. But remember, grandpa-san had left her and her brothers and sisters very well fixed, indeed. I guess I was her favorite charity.

The car started right up, much to my surprise. I was almost certain that I had run the battery down the night of the earthquake. But she turned over right away, loyal little machine that she is, and I was off to the Point to meet the lady with the fixed smile.

And she was smiling as she opened the door to Felicia Montalvo's splendid house. Smiling, though, with a certain coldness in her eyes. I know she didn't look a bit like Jack Nicholson, but there was something of "The Joker" about her. A certain malevolence, masked by that persistent smile.

"Come in, Mr. Riordan. Please. Into the living room. I need to talk to you."

I followed her and watched as she sat down with some small ceremony on a couch. I took a chair opposite her.

"So, what can I do for you, Mrs. Rutledge? Remember I'm wounded, so I can't go after any dragons. Why did you call me here?"

"My son . . . ," she began, as if disbelieving what she was about to say. "My son has disappeared." For a moment, I thought I saw a slight downturn at the corners of that smile, but maybe I was mistaken.

"I thought he was in the county jail, ma'am. They rarely let people disappear from the county jail."

"I provided his bail money. He was released in my custody almost before he could be photographed and fingerprinted. I am responsible for him. Last night he went to bed upstairs, and this morning when I looked in, he was gone. What clothes he had with him were gone. His stepfather's car was gone."

"Mrs. Rutledge, I am in no shape to help you. Have you called the sheriff?"

"No . . . no, I don't want the authorities to know yet. You understand. It's not the bail money. I'd forfeit it all in a moment, if I only knew where he went."

Motherhood must be a wonderful thing. Young Jason Andrews had been arrested because his mother accused him of killing his stepfather. The sheriff's people jail him because he had plenty of motive and no alibi. Then mama bails the kid out and takes him home. Then he cuts out. And now she wanted me to do . . . what? I'm not a particularly violent man, but if Jason had come through the door just at that moment, I would have been tempted to take him down to Point Lobos and feed him to a loitering shark. With my luck, though, there wouldn't be any sharks around.

I decided to play it cool. "What kind of car did Jason take?"

"It was a Cadillac Brougham. His stepfather never drove anything but Cadillacs."

"Any other cars in the garage? I mean, you have to have some transportation, don't you?"

"I really don't know what's in the garage. Harrison's car was parked in the driveway. I haven't looked in the garage since I came up from Los Angeles. It just didn't occur to me."

"Can we take a look, please?" I was beginning to feel that little surge in the chest that comes to me when I'm about to stumble onto something.

She nodded, and led the way through the dining room and kitchen to the inside door opening into the garage.

"It's dark in here. Do you know where the light switch is?" I stumbled and banged my bad arm up against something.

The lights went up. It was a big garage. There was an oil-stained space where the Cadillac, I guess, was customarily parked. And alongside the space was a black pickup truck, sprung high, with oversize tires.

"Yours, Mrs. Rutledge?"

"I've never seen it before," she said. And somehow, I was inclined to believe her.

31

"Masuda and Riordan, may I help you?"

WHAT DOES the intelligent investigator do when he spots a vehicle suspected of being involved in a recent attempted murder? He feels the hood, man. Which is what I did. It was warm, almost hot to the touch. The pickup had not been in the garage very long.

"You've never seen this truck before, Mrs. Rutledge? Never before? You've been here in the house for several days now, and you've never seen this vehicle before?"

"Believe what you like, Mr. Riordan. This is the first time I've laid eyes on this ugly thing."

"In the past thirty minutes, where have you been?"

"Right here. In this room. Telephoning your office."

"The garage door. Doesn't it make a noise when it goes up and down? Most of 'em do."

"I really have no idea. I have never operated the garage door."

"Operated? Then it's on a remote opening thing, right?"

"Yes, I believe so. I think Harrison told me that. But I was never given a device to open it. I never had to. Harrison. . . ."

"Your husband had a remote device. Anybody else?"

The lady had been smiling that relentless smile all during this conversation. A small tic had developed at the outside corner of her left eye. Her hands were tightly clasped together at her breastbone, and she looked at me constantly without blinking.

"I . . . do . . . not . . . know. Please, let's go back in the house. It's cold out here."

It wasn't really cold. Colder than inside, sure. But inside was almost uncomfortably hot. Stephanie Rutledge, however, was very pale. This is a very complicated woman, I thought. We went back into the house.

"Did your husband do any business out of this place, Mrs. Rutledge?"

"I suppose he did. He usually took care of everything by phone or FAX. He had a room upstairs fitted out as an office."

"Let's see it."

She led the way. I remembered climbing those stairs for the first time at the summons of Felicia Montalvo. The first door at the top led into the high-ceilinged room Felicia had used as a studio. On the occasion of my first visit, the room was dominated by a huge easel in the center, and a giant window and skylight on the north side. As Mrs. Rutledge led me into that same room three years later, I was struck by the vast difference in atmosphere.

The skylight was covered by a sort of blind drawn tightly across it. The huge window was covered by a heavy drape. The easel, of course, was gone. The room was sparsely furnished: a desk, a FAX machine, a four-line phone, a waste basket. Papers in disarray spread across the desk. A bank of three-drawer filing cabinets against one wall, with one drawer half way open.

"That must have happened in the earthquake." Stephanie's voice was almost inaudible. "I haven't had time to take stock of damage. I'm surprised there's not a lot of damage. It was such a violent shock."

I started to examine the materials on the desk. Nothing of any real consequence. Bills, copies of correspondence, bank statements and the like. The drawers of the desk yielded very little. *Except* a couple of remote control devices that I figured must be for the garage.

"OK, let's go downstairs. I want to try something."

Silently and meekly, she led me back down the staircase to the ground level.

I handed her one of the remotes. "I'm going to stay in here with the telephone. You go out with this thing and operate the garage door. It's very simple. You just stand at the curb and press this button. I want to see what happens."

Obediently, she went out the front door. I waited inside. I picked up the phone and called my office. Reiko answered: "Masuda and Riordan, may we help you?"

"Ah, so you're taking top billing these days, when the old man is *hors de combat*. That isn't very nice."

"I just get tired of answering the other way. Anyhow, being the *senior* partner doesn't make you the more *important* partner. What's up? Where are you?"

"I'm at the Rutledge house, reconstructing a situation. Pay attention and you'll learn something. I found that big black pickup truck in the Rutledge garage. The smiling blonde lady claims she never saw it before. The damn' thing tried to eat me an hour ago, and she never saw it before. So I'm trying to find out how it could have got back into the garage without her knowing it. It was still hot when I touched it."

"Why call me? What can I do?"

"Number one, *she* told me she called you from this room. Number two, you can't do anything. Just sit there. In rapt admiration of your senior partner."

I heard a voice in the room behind me: "Mr. Riordan, I did what you asked me to do. I opened the garage door and closed it several times. Did you hear anything?"

"Talk to you later," I said to the phone, and hung up.

Stephanie stood there smiling and twitching. "Well, did you hear anything?"

The fact is that I hadn't heard a squeak nor a thump.

"Are you sure you made it go up and down several times?"

She sat down wearily. "Yes, yes, yes. I know what you were trying to do. You really didn't believe me when I told you that I had never seen that machine before. You didn't think somebody else could have put it back in the garage without my hearing something. Are you satisfied?"

I felt a little sheepish. "Mind if I try?" was all I could think to say.

She handed me the device. I walked out to the street and pressed the button. The garage door went up, and it didn't make a sound. I walked nearer, and pressed the button again. The door went down silently. I opened the thing again and walked into the garage.

My old friend Felicia Montalvo had apparently installed the quietest and most efficient garage door opener known to man. But she didn't stop there. For the first time, I noticed that the garage wall next to the

house was considerably thicker than the outside wall, and was probably heavily insulated.

I had to conclude that Stephanie Rutledge had been telling at least
part of the truth. She *couldn't* have heard somebody pull in the garage
with the pickup. But I wasn't at all sure that she hadn't seen it before.

32

"He ran out of gas?"

WHAT ABOUT MY SON?'' she asked. There were tears in her voice, if not in her eyes. "That's what I called you for. What are you going to do?"

"What you should have done right away. I'm going to call the sheriff's office. What's the license number of the Cadillac?"

Reluctantly, she gave it to me as I punched out the sheriff's phone number. "Is Sergeant Balestreri there? Pat Riordan calling."

"I'm sorry, he's not. Could someone else help you?"

"Oh, sure, anybody. I've got a fugitive report."

"Fugitive? I'm not sure what you mean."

"I mean I'm reporting a bail jumper and information about how to catch him. How does that sound?"

"Well, you needn't get sarcastic about it." The young woman at the other end had taken offense at my tone. Well, I guess I was pretty snotty. And my arm was beginning to ache like hell.

"Sorry, sweetie. Just put me in touch with anybody."

"I'll connect you with Lieutenant Hardaway."

I had had several occasions to talk to Hardaway. He always sounded like a gentle soul who couldn't bear to see even a criminal suffer. But

Balestreri had told me that the man was as his name suggested, a hard rock. "Probably the best cop in the county. Besides me, of course," he often says.

"Hardaway here," came the soft voice of the Lieutenant.

"This is Pat Riordan."

"Oh, sure, Riordan, how can I help you?"

"You had a murder suspect named Jason Andrews. He was bailed out by his mother. He has skipped, driving his stepfather's Cadillac. The license number is. . . ."

"We got him, Riordan. His car ran out of gas down near Rocky Point. One of our cruisers stopped to help him and found the kid leaning on the steering wheel, crying his eyes out. He offered no resistance. Identified himself, and was taken into custody. He's back in jail now. Does that help?"

"He ran out of gas?" I was dumfounded.

"Yeah. I guess he was in a panic when he took off. Didn't even look at the gas gauge. Pretty dumb, huh?"

"Thanks, Lieutenant. I'll tell his mother. I'm sure she'll be relieved."

I put the phone down and turned to Stephanie. "The boy is safe. He's in jail. He ran out of gas." I still couldn't believe it.

Her face was trying to express happiness that her son was alive and well. But all the scar tissue was holding it in that scary grimace. She sat down, and for the first time I could see the grayish roots of her blonde hair.

I felt a surge of pity for the woman. "Can I get you a drink of water or something?"

She shook her head. "No, thank you. I appreciate your help. Now, if you don't mind, I'd like to be alone for a while. I've got to sort out some things in my mind."

"OK. Call me if you need me. Here, this is my number at home." I scribbled it down on a pad by the phone.

Stephanie Rutledge was sitting quietly on her couch when I left. I still wasn't sure about her. But there was nothing I could do at the moment. I got in the Mercedes and started home.

The streets on Carmel Point are all curved and irregular by design, I guess. Or maybe they just evolved that way. They're narrow, too. And you've got to be pretty careful as you drive.

One of those monstrous motor home things loomed up ahead of me, barely moving. Another tourist, I thought, doesn't know where he is and doesn't know where he's going. They get out here and get lost. Then the vehicle stopped dead ahead of me.

A spry little man in shorts, nude from the waist up, was raking leaves at the berm. The driver of the monstrosity was apparently asking directions. I sat, patiently, unable to move. I sat, and sat. Finally, after about two minutes of great patience, I honked my horn. The thing didn't move. The spry little man appeared to be engaged in an animated conversation with the invisible driver.

At long last, the vehicle lumbered forward. I got out from behind him at the next cross street, frustrated and angry. Somehow, I must have got turned around, because I found myself in front of the Rutledge house once again. But something had changed. In the driveway was silver Jaguar, sleek and shiny, with a Los Angeles Rams sticker on the rear bumper. Mrs. Rutledge had a visitor.

I drove down a few houses and parked against a hedgerow. On foot I approached the Rutledge place with the vague notion of peeping in the window, I guess. There wasn't any other way. I *had* to know who Stephanie's visitor was.

As quietly as possible, I sneaked up to what I thought was a living room window, and peered into the kitchen whose walls were still covered with Felicia Montalvo's paintings. Wrong place. I moved carefully to another window and stared into the dining room. I am not good at Peeping Tomism. Then I froze as I heard the unmistakable sound of the front door opening. From behind a convenient shrub I was able to observe Stephanie Rutledge being escorted to the lately arrived Jaguar by a tall, swarthy, dangerous-looking man who had to be Eddie Colucci.

33

Why the hell was I doing this, anyhow?

COLUCCI WAS tall and dark complexioned. He wore a tailored suit so obviously expensive that he couldn't afford to gain half a pound anywhere. He carried a large brown folder under his arm.

Stephanie allowed the man to open the car door and gallantly assist her into the Jaguar. She appeared to be in a sort of trance. Neither person spoke a word.

The car backed carefully out of the driveway and pulled out on the narrow street. I bolted for the Mercedes as they drove away in a northerly direction. Before they could get out of my sight, I was following them.

The Jaguar turned east on Santa Lucia and headed up the hill, with me behind it at a respectable distance. I've never had a problem following people in the Mercedes. Nobody in this world would suspect that a private detective would try to shadow him in a Mercedes. Shabby, nondescript domestic automobiles, that's what PIs use.

Colucci turned right onto Rio Road and started down the hill past the Mission. As I followed, I kept guessing which way he'd turn at the intersection of Highway One. To my mild surprise, he didn't turn either way. He waited out the long red light, and drove straight ahead on Rio Road.

All of us in these parts know that the lights on this bottom stretch of Rio Road are notoriously out of sync. Colucci hit both red ones, with me two cars back. Finally, he turned left, past the post office and right almost immediately into the parking area of one of the large office buildings that have sprung up here in recent years. I drove on by and parked in the lot near the Barnyard, a collection of boutiques, and restaurants.

Walking briskly back to the building into which my quarry had disappeared, I nonchalantly entered the lobby. Neither Colucci nor Mrs. Rutledge was in sight. I may have screwed up, I said to myself. I should have stayed closer.

On the wall was a directory of tenants. I scanned it, hoping for some sort of inspiration. Quite a few brokerages, most of 'em with well-known names. Some real estate outfits. A copying establishment. They could have gone there, maybe. But then I remembered that there was a copying machine in Rutledge's upstairs office. I had to use the good old-fashioned process of elimination.

"Rumford and Rumford, Attorneys. Charles L. Menninger, CPA. Henry Wilcox, CPA. Arlo Langston, CLU." I read all these things aloud to myself. "What the hell's a CLU?" I said to nobody in particular. A severe-looking young woman nearby gave me a withering glance. "C&R Investments. MADD. The National Rifle Association. Why do *they* have an office here? Wait a minute. C&R Investments. Colucci and Rutledge, maybe?" I noted the floor and the number and took off up the stairs. In buildings of four floors or less, I always use the stairs. Aside from climbing the Sixth Avenue hill, it's the only exercise I get. Running upstairs: great for the cardiovascular system.

As I slowed to a walk on the second landing, I began to doubt my own instincts. What if I were wrong? What if I picked the wrong company? Why the hell was I doing this, anyhow?

When I approached the office of C&R Investments, my anxiety eased up a little. I could see shadows moving behind the barely translucent glass of the office door. Of course, they could have been *any* shadows, but I had a hunch I had found the right place. I looked around for a place to wait for Stephanie and Colucci to come out. There wasn't any.

I was in a modern, undecorated hall. At one end was the door leading to the stairway I had just ascended. In the middle was an elevator door.

Arranged on both sides of the corridor were offices, all alike, all of a size. There was no nook or cranny for me to hide in. If I went back through the stairway door, I couldn't observe the C&R office.

At the far end of the hall was a window looking out on the range of hills that rises up at the mouth of Carmel Valley. I *could* be gazing out the window when Mrs. Rutledge and her sometime amour came out. But why the hell would anybody be gazing out the window for more than a minute and a half?

While I was debating with myself, the door to C&R Investments opened. I hastily turned to the window. In its reflection I could dimly see three figures emerge. If they knew that another person was in the hall, they gave no sign. They moved directly to the elevator, waited a few moments for the car, and entered. I dashed down the hall to watch the little arrow go down.

So far my surveillance had been in vain, and I was beginning to wonder why I undertook it in the first place. I've got to say, despite my natural modesty, that I'm really very good at what I do. But sometimes I do things that I cannot explain, even to myself.

Running down the stairs and trying to pick up the trail on those three people seemed more than futile. It suddenly struck me as a kind of low comedy. Who were the three figures I saw in the fuzzy, distorted reflection in the window? I had immediately assumed that they were Stephanie Rutledge, Colucci, and somebody else. But what somebody else? I couldn't even tell if the third person was tall and thin or short and fat. For that matter, male or female.

I was standing in the middle of the hallway, scratching my head. Directly behind me was the C&R Investments door. I turned and gave the knob a twist. The door was locked. Calling upon the old tricks I learned when but a novice, under the tutelage of a crusty old PI who swore he was a close friend of Dash Hammett, I picked the lock with a small tool I carry for the purpose, and went in.

C&R Investments was contained in one room. Some file cabinets, a couple of chairs, a bare desk with a telephone. Nothing else. Two people went in, three people came out.

I pulled out all the desk drawers. Empty. I pulled out the drawers of the file cabinets. Likewise. I looked out the window just in time to see Colucci's Jaguar disappear around the corner on Rio Road. I would have kicked myself in the ass if I could have got the proper angle. But just then I smelled something.

Yeah, smelled something. Very common, very familiar smell. I pulled the wastebasket out from under the desk and found the source of the odor. A sheaf of papers, now mostly ashes, were still smoldering. I dumped the stuff out on the cheap institutional carpet and stamped out the sparks. Not a hell of a lot left. The corners of a couple of sheets of paper had not burned yet, but I could tell what they had been attached to. The form was standard and easily recognizable. The charred papers in the wastebasket had been some sort of legal document. In a moment of inspiration, or revelation, or epiphany, or something, I knew that it was the last will and testament of Harrison Rutledge.

34

"Of course, I am not a <u>real</u> policeman."

OF COURSE, I couldn't prove that it was Rutledge's will. All I had were a couple of pieces of paper with charred edges; enough to identify the legal nature of the document, but no name, no heirs.

It might have gone like this: Colucci and Stephanie planned to kill Rutledge, lay the blame on Farnham, and waltz off with all the loot. When Farnham became too cagey for them, they decided to frame poor Jason Andrews who, besides being emotionally unstable, was also decidedly unbright. So far, so good. But what if Rutledge's will cut Stephanie out? They'd have to find it and destroy all copies. Which they were in the process of doing. I thought.

But, then, why the hell would somebody want to kill *me?* And there was the problem of Felicia Montalvo's hidden treasure that got me involved in the first place.

I stuffed the fragments of paper into a jacket pocket, and went down in the elevator. You don't get any exercise walking *down* stairs, only *up.*

The wound in my shoulder was healing rapidly, although it made me wince from time to time. Especially when I forgot about it and tried to do something like opening the car door with my right hand. I eased myself behind the wheel of the Mercedes, and tried to get comfortable. There was nobody to chase, so I took my own sweet time getting back over to Monterey.

Reiko was entertaining a visitor when I walked into the office. She's been seeing a lot of Greg Farrell lately. He's the shaggy Big Sur artist I've told you about before. I thought at first Reiko's guest was Greg. But when the guy turned around, I could see that he was respectably dressed in a suit and tie, garments that Farrell wouldn't be caught dead in, and that he was obviously Asian. My God, I thought, another one of her clan that I haven't seen before.

"Pat Riordan meet Sab Morita, my second cousin, twice removed. He's with the. . . ."

"Glendale police. Yeah, I know. You told me. Nice to know you, Sab. What brings you to Monterey?"

"This whole Rutledge thing. Reiko's told you, I'm sure, that we've had the guy under surveillance for weeks. Somebody tipped us that he was running a high level narcotics business from his house. When we got word that he had been murdered, it seemed like a good notion to come up and find out first-hand what happened. The wife fingered her own kid, Rutledge's stepson, I understand. Then she bailed him out. He tried to skip, and the county people picked him up. That about right?"

"That's about as much as I know. Anything else I *ought* to know?"

"We know about Colucci, too. He's up here someplace, we think. Can you tell me anything about him?"

"This is your lucky day, Sab. Colucci picked up Stephanie Rutledge at the Rutledge house on Carmel Point about an hour and a half ago. I followed them to an office down on Carmel Rancho Boulevard. They left the office with another guy, but I didn't see the third person well enough to identify him. I checked out the office and found this in the wastebasket." I hauled out the scraps of paper with the charred edges.

"So, what's with the paper?"

"Looks to me like it might have been what was left of a will that they were trying to burn."

Detective Morita examined the fragments of paper, turning them over and over, but he just looked puzzled. "Why a will? Looks like a legal document, all right. But couldn't it have been a contract or a bill of sale or something?"

I felt injured. "It *could* have been a marriage license, maybe. But my best instincts tell me that it was one copy of the will of Harrison

Rutledge, and that Stephanie and Colucci were trying to get rid of it so that they could share Rutledge's estate and live in perpetual bliss. Of course, I am not a *real* policeman."

"Hold on, Riordan. I didn't mean to hurt your feelings. Your're probably right. Let's go on that assumption. Hey, I know you've been around a lot longer than I have. I've got to trust your experience."

I looked at Sab Morita. He is probably the tallest Japanese I ever met, an inch or two over six feet, coal black hair, and a round, unlined face that could light up with a smile that was the equal of Reiko's on her happiest days. Maybe he is a lot younger than I am. There's just no way of telling. Reiko doesn't look a minute older than the day I met her ten years ago.

"Thank you for your vote of confidence. Since you are some kind of relative of my partner, I forgive you. Now you know what I know. Reiko has probably filled you in on all the other details. What's police procedure in Glendale in a case like this?"

"Well, we're not the homicide capital of Southern California, you know, but we have our share. And I suggest that we get with the local constabulary and put all our facts on the table. First, though, where do you think we can find Stephanie Rutledge?"

"Back at the house on the Point. Being the grieving widow. Still selling the story that her son killed her husband. Probably being consoled by Eddie Colucci, an old friend of the family. Oh, yeah, and this is for you, too, Reiko: In the garage of the Rutledge home is the mean-looking modified giant pickup that tried to run me down today a couple of blocks from my house in Carmel. Stephanie claims never to have seen the vehicle before."

Reiko perked up. "The truck the guy shot you from? Same one tried to splatter you on the street?"

" 'From which the guy shot me.' Better English, Reiko-san. It seems to be so. From descriptions I have heard of the truck, I think it's a match. Wicked looking goddam thing."

"Tell you what," said Morita, "let's all get into my rented car, and you show me how to get to the Rutledge house. 'The Point', you say. What is that?"

"It's a little piece of territory outside the jurisdiction of the Carmel police on a sharp corner of this rocky Peninsula. In recent years, people have been building very large houses on very small lots until there just isn't a hell of a lot of space left. But you don't want to get me going on the subject of local real estate."

"I'll have to trust you to show me the way, Riordan. Let's go."

We filed down the stairs to the street and up to a public parking garage on Calle Principal. Morita's car was a shiny new Chevrolet with every conceivable extra. All it lacked was a wet bar and a TV. When I looked at him inquisitively, he said, with a note of apology in his voice, "The department insists that we go first class. But remember, the is just a *Chevrolet*." It was half again as big as the 1950 Bel Air coupe, which was the first car I ever owned. Bought it after I got out of the Army in '53. It was a hardtop, y'know. Cute as hell, and rugged as an army jeep. "Just a *Chevrolet*," indeed. I climbed into the back seat and let Reiko ride shotgun.

I guided Morita over Carmel Hill on Highway One, and down the other side to Rio Road. There I turned him right on Rio and left at the Mission, down around the Mission Ranch, where I found my first murder victim in these parts, and out Fifteenth Avenue to Carmel Point. A left and a right and a left and we were at the house.

"There. It doesn't look like a hell of a lot, but it would probably bring between $850K and a million two, depending on the realtor and the time of year. I have no idea how much Rutledge paid for it. But according to the guy who sold it to him, it didn't seem to matter."

We parked and got out. Morita hesitated for a moment, but Reiko marched straight up the walk to the front door and banged the knocker. The door opened, and we were greeted by the lady with the permanent smile.

"Hello, there. We've been expecting you, Mr. Riordan. And you, too, detective. Sorry I don't know your name. But I've certainly seen you around. And the little lady, too. You're all welcome. Come in."

35

"Did you unearth any deep, dark secrets?"

THE GRACIOUS, ever-so-proper Mrs. Rutledge led us into the living room. Eddie Colucci stood by the fireplace with a tall drink in his hand. He seemed perfectly at ease. Now that I had a chance to study the man close up, I could see that he was a good-looking bastard, with the kind of animal appeal that dangerous men often have. He was about forty-five or fifty or somewhere in between, and he was comfortable in his very expensive suit which, as I have said, was cut so close he couldn't have been concealing a gun anywhere. He looked like a successful business man which, I'm sure he would tell you, he was.

"Won't you please find seats? And can I get anyone a drink?" said Stephanie. She was as cool as Colucci. It was as though we had all been invited to a little party, and the hostess could think of nothing but making us comfortable.

I could see that Reiko and her cousin were uneasy. They both had those embarrassed Japanese smiles and offered quick little bows as they refused the drinks. I, on the other hand, decided to go along with the spirit of the occasion.

"Got any 7-Up? Sorry, but that's all I drink. That and coffee. Maybe a hot cup of coffee? By the way, Mr. Colucci and I haven't been properly introduced. Hi, Eddie, I'm Pat Riordan. I've seen you around."

The man's expression did not change. He lounged against the mantelpiece, acknowledged my greeting by raising his glass as if toasting me, and took a long draft of his drink.

"I'm sorry, Mr. Riordan. We have no 7-up, and there's no coffee. I could make some if. . . ."

"Oh, please, don't go to any trouble. Let's get right to the point. Let me present my partner, Reiko Masuda, and Sergeant Sab Morita of the Glendale police. You said you had been expecting us. May I inquire why?" I've never been so goddam polite in my life.

"Mr. Colucci noticed you following us as we drove over Santa Lucia. He's . . . he's something of an expert at that sort of thing. He's *used* to being followed. And he can spot a tail—as he phrases it—very quickly. We were also aware of you in the hall as we left the office. We had no doubt that you would show up here, although I wasn't expecting you so soon."

Colucci was jingling some change or keys in his pocket and taking frequent sips from his drink, which I noticed was particularly long and especially dark and contained no ice at all.

"What's he drinking? It's the color of sloe gin, which is nauseating stuff."

Colucci smiled. "It's Coca Cola, Riordan, if it's any of your business. In Vegas, when we run a club, we don't drink. We like to see the customers drink, because it makes them reckless. But I don't drink alcohol at all. Not on or off the job." His voice was deep and soft, but there was steel in it. He was a pro, no doubt, and he was affirming it.

"Well, Mr. Riordan, have you any explanation for your following us? Did you unearth any deep, dark secrets?" Stephanie sat on the arm of my chair and put her hand on my good shoulder.

"I found an empty office. A dummy. A mail drop. A front. And I am truly curious about why a mythical corporation like C&R Investments should maintain an office in Carmel, California, a place of unmatched serenity." I thought it prudent to withhold for the moment the fact that I found the burned documents.

"I'll let Mr. Colucci explain. Eddie, if you please."

Reiko and Sab sat quietly, content to let me carry the ball. Colucci placed his drink on the mantel and walked deliberately to the middle of the room. I felt an uncomfortable pang in my gut. This guy is used to taking charge, I said to myself, and he's going to be a hard nut to crack. He cleared his throat. I listened.

"Harrison—the late Mr. Rutledge—and I were partners in a successful operation in Las Vegas. We were survivors, actually. There were several more interested parties in the beginning, but one by one they dropped out. Some just signed over their shares and left town. Others, unfortunately, died. Of course, we saw to it that they got appropriate floral tributes.

"Not long ago, Harrison and I had a falling out. Oh, we remained partners in business. But certain *personal* things came between us. Harrison was always wrapped up in business, and neglected this lovely lady here. She and I came to know each other quite well, and this did not please her husband when he found out about our . . . friendship. It was at about that time that Eric Farnham put in an appearance in Glendale with some cockamamey story about Felicia Montalvo's lost fortune.

"We all knew Felicia, of course. And we knew the old witch was loaded. It wasn't hard to buy Farnham's story about the treasure that must have been hidden somewhere in Carmel Point. Harrison and I agreed that we should buy the place, and that he would establish residence there to learn where the money was. Farnham was to have a share of anything we turned up.

"But apparently Farnham decided to operate on his own. He hired you, Riordan, to help him. As far as we can determine, you've had no success. That so?"

I nodded, fascinated. It was like the reverse of a detective story, where the detective gathers all the suspects together, weaves all the clues into a damning conclusion and points out the guilty party. Only here it was one of the criminals doing the weaving, while the representatives of law and order sat silent.

"As for Harrison's death, we are convinced that Jason, Stephanie's son by a former marriage, out of insanity brought on by his natural hatred for his stepfather, killed him. That about rounds out the story, doesn't it?"

I glanced at Stephanie. She was smiling that death's-head smile at Colucci, but there appeared to be tears in her eyes. Her thin fingers were interlaced and twisting, her shoulders hunched.

"What about the office?" I asked. "Why an empty office? Didn't Harrison carry on his business from upstairs here? Or do you guys just like to pay rent in an expensive building because you feel sorry for Carmel landlords?"

"I'm glad you asked that question," he said. But I could see he wasn't. "We had intended to use the office for certain operations we hoped to have going here, but unfortunately it never came to pass."

"That's interesting. Then who was the guy who came out of the office with you when I was in the hall? I was looking out the window, but I'm sure I saw the reflection of *three* people going into the elevator. Who was the third person?"

There was an exchange of glances between Colucci and Mrs. Rutledge. "What third person?" he asked, after a pause. "There was no other person. Just Stephanie and me. Just two of us. You must have been mistaken."

36

"I saw three people, goddamit!"

WE WERE ON our way back to Monterey. Nobody had said a word. Finally, Sab spoke up:

"So what did we learn that we didn't know already?"

Neither Reiko nor I had an answer for that one. We *had* met Colucci, although that didn't really mean anything. We all had known who and what Colucci was. The only new wrinkle was the bare-faced lie that was laid on us by Colucci *and* Stephanie about the third party I saw coming out of the office.

Now, my eyesight is very sharp in the middle and long distances. Not so good for telephone books, menus, and my watch. That's why I carry these little drug store glasses in my pocket most of the time. They only cost eight or nine bucks, so there's no great loss when I lose them, which I always do. But in the hall of that office building, in broad daylight, with the aid of a lot of fluorescent tubes recessed in the ceiling, I know damn well I saw three people in that window reflection. True, I couldn't identify the third party, nor could I tell if it was male or female. But it was *there*. That meant that, despite Colucci's cool self-control and plausible explanation, there was a big old nasty lie at the center of things.

"They were lying, you know. When they told us they were the only people in that office. More liars, more goddam liars. Lies to cover up murders, and lies to cover up other lies. I saw three people come out of that office. I didn't see them clearly, but I saw 'em. Let there be no doubt about that."

"You could have been mistaken, Riordan," said Reiko in a quiet voice. "You know, like there wasn't much time, and you didn't want to be seen yourself. You said you had to duck your head into the window when they came out. It's a wonder you didn't break the glass."

"*I saw three people, goddammit!* Period. End of argument. They got into the elevator. All I ever saw after that was the top of Colucci's Jaguar. But I *know* what I *saw.*"

"OK, OK, OK. I didn't mean to hurt your feelings. So stick pins in me. You saw three people come out of C&R Investments. How come you didn't mention finding the burned papers?"

"Have you no shame, Reiko? This is just one more thing you have to learn about this business. *Never* show your hole card until you can use it. *Wakarimasu-ka?*"

"*Wakarimasu.* So what are you going to do with your 'hole card'?"

"Damned if I know."

Sab Morita had not spoken during the trip. Not until we were going down Cass Street in Monterey did he open his mouth: "Maybe I can help. Either of you know of a private investigator named Garcia from East L.A.?"

That shook us both up. "Do we know Angel Garcia? Come on, Sab, what's the connection? Garcia's still up here somewhere. He works for the Rutledges. Big guy? Mustache? Are we talking about the same man?"

Morita took a long deep breath. "You know him. You've talked to him. What has he told you?"

"First he told us he came up here looking for Eric Farnham. Said he was conducting the search for a lady in Glendale who had a romantic interest in Farnham. Then later he told us he had worked for Rutledge for a long time, as a sort of bag man. *Then* he showed up at my house with Jason Andrews, the stepson of Rutledge, who accused me of all sorts of crimes and misdemeanors. Finally, he suggested to me that the Rutledge *daughter,* a runaway, had shot me. And God knows a lot of other things I cannot remember at this time. Why?"

"Angel, as you might have deduced, is *not* an angel. He talks out of both sides of his mouth, occasionally out of his nostrils, and, for all I know, out of his asshole. He is the trickiest of tricksters, and he doesn't know right from wrong. Whatever he might have told you probably has a grain or two of truth in it, but only the grain or two that would be useful to Angel. Are you following me?"

We were hanging on his words, both of us, and he knew it. He glanced over at me. "Is this where I turn? I don't know where we are."

Reiko spoke up: "Bear left here. Now watch the traffic coming from the right. OK, left now. This is Alvarado. Keep talking."

"Angel was more than a bag man for Rutledge and Colucci. He had a piece of the action. *He* was the guy who was originally sent out to dispose of Farnham. Oh, that's in our files too, Riordan. Remember, Rutledge lived in Glendale for a long time. We've followed his movements for years. And we've been very much aware of Angel Garcia. He kept his little office in East L.A. and logged just enough legitimate business to back up the fact that he's a private investigator. We were never able to get enough on him to bust him, or even take his license. But he's a bad apple. Does that help? Could it have been Garcia with Mrs. Rutledge and Colucci?"

I thought about it. The third figure. I closed my eyes and tried to get the picture back, the three figures emerging from the office I saw reflected in the glass. They crossed the hall, one of 'em pushed the elevator call button, they got in the elevator and went down. It all happened in a matter of seconds. The elevator must have been stopped at their floor.

"No. No, it wasn't Garcia. I'd seen Garcia a number of times. I'd have recognized the figure, even if I couldn't see the face. He's a big man. The third figure in the group I saw was an ordinary sized person. Like me."

"Hey, here we are," said Reiko. She pointed out our office and guided Morita into a parking space.

The Glendale detective pulled into the curb and turned the key. "No help, eh? Sorry. I can't think of anybody else that might be involved in this business. We know the family, the two kids, Colucci, Garcia. We've been watching 'em for a long time. We know Farnham, too, but he's in jail. Sorry, Riordan." He turned to his cousin. "Reiko, can you put me up for a couple of nights. You got a couch or something?"

"Better, Sab. Uncle Shiro owns my apartment building, and there's a furnished studio empty. He's probably in his office upstairs, I'll run up and check him out." She got out of the car and disappeared up the stairs.

"Honestly, Riordan, is she much help? Hell, when we were kids she used to be the wildest girl on the block. She could easily take out guys twice her size with a couple of karate strokes. Which she had to do, you know, because when she began to blossom, she was also the prettiest kid on the block. But no nonsense, man, no playin' around."

"I didn't know you two lived near each other."

"We didn't for long. Maybe three-four years. Down in Orange County. Before her dad moved to San Jose. But she's somebody you never forget. I only wish she weren't my cousin." He smiled, wistfully.

"I only wish I were twenty years younger." *I* smiled, wistfully.

We got out of the car and walked up the steep stairway to the office. The door was ajar. I guessed that Reiko had unlocked it and then dashed down to her uncle's office to nail down the vacant apartment for Sab. But I was wrong.

My partner was standing there with her hands in the air. Across the room stood Jason Andrews, with a very large gun pointed at all three of us.

37

"You made me mad, Riordan."

ALL I COULD think to say was, "How the hell did you get out?"

Young Jason smiled a nasty smile. His eyes were glittering like the sequins on a stripper's nipples. (Mickey Spillane couldn't do better than that, don't you think?) He really *looked* crazy.

"You thought you could railroad me, did you? You thought that I killed my stepfather. I can tell that you think I'm insane now. Well, you're going to find out just how insane I am." He waved the gun at us. "Now, this is what I want you to do. Just move to your right around the room. I'm keeping an eye on you. That's it, around until you're against the window. I'm moving with you, and I'm watching you. Don't go for a gun or you're dead."

I threw open my jacket. "Do you see a gun here, Jason? I never carry a gun. A gun can go off and kill somebody. Like *your* gun there. There's not even a gun in my desk drawer. Hard to believe, isn't it? A private eye without a gun. Anybody knows that you've got to have a gun to *be* somebody. A *big* gun. That's what makes you a man, right? The guy with the gun is the guy in control. Jason, you're a wimp and a mama's boy. As a matter of fact it's your mama who's trying to get you nailed for the murder of your stepfather, not us."

He looked confused. His jaw had dropped during my little speech, and the maniacal gleam had gone out of his eyes. The gun was pretty heavy and it tilted down in his skinny hand until it was pointed at my desk.

"My mother? My *mother* said I killed that sonofabitch Rutledge? Why did she do that?" His face seemed to be melting like a figure in an overheated wax museum. He backed slowly out of my office and sat on Reiko's desk with the gun dangling almost to the floor. All the fire was gone.

Sab walked calmly up to Jason and took the gun out of his hand. The boy didn't seem to notice.

"Jason, how did you get out? Last I heard, you were in County Jail." I put my hand on his shoulder.

"Somebody bailed me out. I figured it was my mother, but she wasn't there when they turned me loose. Nobody was there. I just caught a cab and came back over here from Salinas."

"Where'd the gun come from?"

"From the house. On the Point. I had the taxi man take me there so I could get my pickup. The gun was on the seat. I'd never seen it before. Then I got real mad. You made me mad, Riordan. You and your snotty attitude. I decided to come over here and. . . ."

"And what, Jason? Kill me? That's going to prove that you *didn't* kill your stepfather?"

He seemed to shrink before our eyes. "I dunno. I dunno what I was gonna do. I'm havin' trouble thinkin'. I'm just sorta. . . ." He looked like he was going to sleep.

"Sab, you're the authority. I think you've got to take over from here. Reiko, you be the guide. Sab, you drive Jason over to the County Jail. Reiko, show him where it is."

All the tension had gone out of the room. Morita took the young man by the arm and led him out. Reiko followed silently. I flopped down in my chair and breathed a long, noisy sigh.

The pickup belonged to Jason. I might have known. A young fellow as insecure as he *would* drive as macho a vehicle as he could find. But it couldn't have been Jason who shot me. Or could it? Who was it that tried to run me down at Sixth and Carpenter in Carmel? How many people had access to that four-wheel-drive assassination machine?

As I have told you before, murder is not my business, except by accident. But when one of these accidents occurs, it always turns out to be a gala affair. Couldn't be a straightforward passion-motivated killing. Oh, no. All my murders have dark corners and secret passages. *But* they contribute a little excitement to my life, I've gotta say that.

Secret passages. Yes, Felicia's money. Caves among the rocks off Carmel Point. Sorry, wrong number. *If* Felicia Montalvo hid her ill-gotten gains around the grounds of her house, or papered her bathroom walls with thousand dollar bills, none of the stuff has shown up yet. But it's got to be there. She rarely left the place. She had no bank account. Like most people who live on the edge, she liked to deal in cash. And Eric Farnham was the guy who should know, if anybody knew, where the loot was hidden.

Now, however, Stephanie Rutledge is living in the house. And Colucci is probably staying there, too. And *they* haven't found anything. If they had, they'd be back in Glendale, abandoning the house, Jason, and the formidable Lisa.

Lisa? Where the hell was she? And what was she doing? Certainly she's not at the Rutledge house. She would have been hanging around when Reiko and Sab and I were there. Back up to Aptos to make up with her failed sculptor? Back down to the fabulous L.A. basin to get lost in the multitudes?

I remembered that it had been suggested that Lisa had shot me. That was Garcia, wasn't it? Then *he* must have known something about that big black pickup with no dog in the back. And he must have known that Lisa could get to it, even though it belonged to her brother.

My right shoulder was beginning to ache again. It comes and it goes. Maybe it was just the thought of that truck and the hard-hatted driver that made it hurt. Or the thought of Lisa Andrews in the leather outfit with the open midriff. Nice navel there. Can't remember if it was an innie or an outie. No matter.

Despite the pain in my shoulder, I started to doze off. I have acquired the ability to slip away for little naps now and then during the day, like Winston Churchill. It's remarkably refreshing. But this time, just as I was drifting away, the phone chirped. I jerked up from my innocent repose, and answered it.

"Yeah," I said.

"Pat, this is Balestreri. You know that kid was bailed out of jail again. How did they do that? This is a murder charge. They aren't supposed to do that."

"That's not my department. I guess they know the right people.

They've got a lot of money. And, besides, I don't think Jason Andrews is a danger to the general population."

"But he tried to run once. What the hell are they thinking of? The sonofabitch tried to skip bail once."

"Tony, you are a big boy and a Detective Sergeant. Why the hell do you call me?"

"Because you're so wrapped up in this thing. You set Farnham up, and he's sitting in jail, charming all the guards. He's got 'em running out for gourmet food. They all think he's the greatest thing since sliced bread. But then, nobody but you and me remember when there *wasn't* any sliced bread. Shit!"

Tony is a couple of years younger than I am. I was a little kid, but I remember my mom sawing away on a loaf with what was known as a "bread knife." Sliced bread was a startling innovation. Like television and computers. The only way it has differed from modern electronic miracles is that it hasn't changed a bit since it was invented.

I changed the subject. "Tony, do you know anything about Lisa Andrews?"

"Who?"

"Lisa Andrews. Rutledge's stepdaughter. Little wiry girl. Young Jason's sister."

"You got me. Where does she fit in?"

"I'm not really sure. She came out of nowhere. Garcia told me she shot me. *She* said she didn't. But she lied about seeing her mother. And she ate all my peanut butter."

"What are you talking about?"

"I don't know. But the dawn is about to break. Bye, Tony."

38

The only sound I could hear was the crying of gulls.

BEFORE I HUNG UP, I assured Balestreri that Jason was on his way back to jail, escorted by Morita and Reiko. He wasn't all that pleased and grumbled something about the little bastard only getting sprung again and what was he doing with a gun, anyhow. I pretended to ignore him.

Innocent little Lisa with the exposed belly-button. She's the very odd piece in this stupid jig-saw puzzle. Why does she always pop into my mind at critical moments? Why do I not trust her? Why do I think she has been lying to me? Why am I rambling like this?

I don't know why. Nor do I know why I got up out of my chair and left the office at that particular moment, carefully locking the door to avoid any further surprises. Lost in my thoughts (mostly of Lisa), I went down the stairs and out into Alvarado Street to look for my car. I couldn't remember where I left it. That's a recurring nightmare that I have. Leaving my car parked on the street or in a large parking lot, and being unable to find it when I need it. Happens about once a month. There I am, wandering around looking for my automobile, knowing that I left it somewhere, *somewhere*. But I never find it—and I wake up. Dumb dream.

But this time I was wide awake, and I *knew* the car was parked nearby, probably with a ticket under the windshield wiper. And, after circumnavigating the block a couple of times, I remembered that I had left it up on Calle Principal in city's covered parking lot.

As I approached the little Mercedes in the dim shadows of the lot, I was once again touched and depressed to see the evidence of violence on my poor machine. Aside from the dents and hints of corrosion, there was the hole in the rear window, the smashed glove compartment. I made a solemn promise to myself to get the thing into a garage as soon as possible, and treat it to a complete renovation. As soon as I had time. As soon as I had the money.

I sat in the car a little while. For once, the meter people had missed me. No citation was on the windshield. I wasted some time adjusting the rear-view mirrors. I became aware for the first time of a dark stain on what was left of the glove compartment lid. Blood. *My* blood. No North Korean, nor any Communist Chinese had drawn my blood. I got mad.

Jamming the car into reverse, I backed noisily out of the space. As anger welled up inside me, I left a little rubber on the concrete as I sped out into Calle Principal, which, fortunately, was empty of traffic at the time.

I headed south to Pearl and up the hill to Pacific, ignoring the speed laws. In that tiny space in the back of my mind that is reserved for intuition, I knew where I was going. I knew what I was going to do. But for the first couple of miles, I didn't know I was being followed once again by a black pickup truck with no dog in the back.

It wasn't until I was racing down Carmel Hill beyond the Ocean Avenue traffic light that I became aware of the follower. Everybody merges into one lane at that point, and out of the corner of my eye I caught a glimpse of that big black evil vehicle fading in behind me as the road narrowed. I made up my mind to give him—or her, or it—a good run for the money. I raced through a yellow light at Rio Road and put the pedal to the floor on Highway One, past the Meadows, past the beach, past Point Lobos, past the Highlands, never looking back. Finally, on a long straight stretch, I glanced into the mirror. About a quarter of a mile behind me was the black pickup.

Maybe I can lose him, I thought, if I can stay this far ahead. A few miles further on I'd get to Greg Farrell's place. If the guy in the pickup couldn't see me, I'd head off the road there and wait.

Sure enough, as I headed down the slope past Palo Colorado Canyon, the truck vanished from my mirror. I did a hard left onto the dirt road at Greg's place and ran back through the high weeds about thirty yards to a stop. I listened for the noise of the pursuing truck.

Nothing. I heard nothing. Either the truck had gone on through when I was crashing through the brush, or it had stopped. Maybe it had given up the chase. Maybe it was half way back to Monterey. And maybe it had flown on by and was on the Bixby Bridge by now.

Greg wasn't home. His ancient rusting truck was gone. I hadn't actually expected to find him, but I'd taken the chance. For some strange reason, probably because we shared the experience of being combat soldiers in different wars, he took it upon himself to rescue me from various forms of danger through the years. I sure could have used him at that moment.

The only sound I could hear was the crying of gulls. It's a noise that never stops along the continent's rim. Even Greg's geese were silent. He calls them his "watch geese." "A hell of a lot better than a dog, Pat," he says. "A dog will wag his tail and run up and lick your hand. These geese are killers. Watch out, don't touch that one, he'll bite." But the geese were asleep, or just ignoring me.

After sitting for at least fifteen minutes, I decided that it was safe to venture out to the highway. Greg's dirt road is a sort of circular driveway, so I started the Mercedes and rolled cautiously through the brush. As I rounded a high growth of weeds I hit the brake and froze. Blocking the opening through which I had come a short while before was the black pickup. Through the tinted windshield I could see that there was nobody at the wheel.

And there I was, without even my blackthorn stick.

39

"You're not as smart as I thought, Riordan."

I HAVE BEEN here before, I thought. Caught in the tall grass and weeds with an enemy somewhere in the immediate neighborhood. Slowly, and as quietly as possible, I got out of the Mercedes, leaving the door open to avoid slamming it. Except for the occasional sound of a fast-moving vehicle on the highway, I couldn't hear anything but gull sounds, wind sounds, surf sounds.

Crouching in the brush, I contemplated my options. There weren't any. If I snuck out on foot and tried to hitch a ride back to Carmel, my pursuer would soon find out I was gone, and it's highly likely that he'd catch up with me before I could catch a ride. I *could* have just crawled further into the weeds and stayed there. But I might have been there for hours, maybe days. No telling where Farrell was. He was as likely to have flown to New York to pitch a gallery as he was to have gone up to Palo Colorado canyon to drink coffee with Ric Masten, the reigning troubador of the Big Sur country.

All I could do was to sneak around and find my adversary before *he* found *me*. I looked around for something I could use as a weapon.

I had just picked up a sturdy-looking stick, when I froze. A voice came from behind me.

"You're not as smart as I thought, Riordan. And that stick is not going to do you any good at all. Turn around slowly, please."

Eddie Colucci stood there with one hand in a pocket of his jacket and the other holding a nasty-looking black automatic.

I put up my hands, still clutching the thick knotted stick I had found in the brush.

"Hello, Eddie. Back to your old trade, huh. Or, maybe, just keeping in practice?"

"Oh, I'm not the guy who's been trying to kill you. I'm just the guy who's going to finish the job. You gave me quite a chase, friend. For a while I thought I'd lost you. Went past here about half a mile. Then, when it dawned on me that you must have turned off somewhere, I turned around and came back. You left a little rubber on the road when you turned in here. It was easy to spot. It's just one of those little things you pick up when you're in my business."

He looked so goddam smug. A true professional who has made contract murder into a science. I just stood there, wondering what to do next. Colucci started walking towards me.

I threw my stick at him with all the force I could muster. When he ducked, it gave me just enough time to dash back into the weeds and start circling around behind him to get to Greg's house. Maybe I thought I could get to the phone and dial 911 or something. Frankly, I wasn't thinking much at the time.

Colucci fired into the brush behind me a couple of times, and then I could hear him crashing after me. I ran up the hill to Greg's fenced-in geese preserve. The startled birds began making noises that could be heard in Monterey. I fell or slid down the dirt bank to the house and crawled in through an open window. Inside, on my hands and knees, I paused to catch my breath.

I could hear Colucci thrashing around in the high weeds. Sooner or later, he'd figure out that I had got into the house. There wasn't a hell of a lot of time. I looked around the room.

The bedroom, where I had landed, is at the back of the house. The telephone is in the front. No 911. Dumb idea in the first place. Then, my gaze fell on something that I thought I would never use again. On the bedside table, in plain sight and probably loaded, was one of Greg's guns.

It didn't take me long to reach the piece. It gave me comfort in my hour of need. And while I had sworn long ago that I'd never use a gun again, the situation I was in called for desperate measures. And with my demonstrated lack of skill with hand guns, this was *truly* desperate.

"Riordan! You in there? If you are, you bastard, come on out, or I'll blast you out. I'll come in there and blow your brains all over the place. This is a forty-five, baby. It makes a lot of noise, but nobody's going to hear it down here. Come on out, or I'm coming in!"

I kept quiet. There was a foot-locker a few feet away. I crawled over to it and stood it up on its end in line with the front of the house. It was pretty heavy, although I couldn't imagine what was in it. But Greg, I know, is a collector of significant junk. Anyway, the thing would furnish protection for a matter of minutes, at least.

Colucci opened the front door. The house is pretty much in a straight line, but it jogs a couple of times and I couldn't see him yet. I heard him, though, walking deliberately, stopping now and then to look into places where he thought I might be hiding.

In what seemed to me to be a long, long time, he reached the bedroom door.

"Stop, Eddie," I said. "I'm armed now. If you come a step forward, *I'll* blast *you.*"

"Bullshit, Riordan. You're bluffing." His eyes were combing the room for me. He didn't seem to notice the upended foot-locker in the middle of the floor with me behind it.

"No, Eddie, I'm not bluffing. I've got the drop on you." I lied. I couldn't see him, but I knew exactly where he was.

He must have discovered me by the sound of my voice. He started firing at the foot-locker, and the slugs tore into it. One of 'em found a soft spot and went right through it, missing my head by a couple of inches.

I put my arm around the box and fired once, in what I dearly hoped would be the right direction. It was. I heard Colucci grunt, groan, and sigh before he hit the floor. I had shot the man. And hurt him enough to put him out of action. Maybe, I thought, I killed him.

A lot of things came back to me in a rush. The first time I fired my rifle in Korea. The first time I ever really saw the enemy soldier I shot. The blood-covered face of the next man I had to kill. I was seized with the shakes. For a couple of minutes I couldn't move.

I got to my feet and walked to the fallen Colucci. He was still breathing, as far as I could see. My bullet had taken him in the gut, and there was a lot of blood on his expensive tailored shirt, spreading out on his expensive Rodeo Drive suit. I pulled the sheet off Greg's bed, made a compress out of it, and put it over the wound. I tied a strip of the sheet around the man's body to keep pressure on the compress.

Then I trotted to the telephone and dialed 911.

50

"You claim it was self-defense. Right?"

COLLUCI WASN'T DEAD. My bullet (or maybe I should say Greg's bullet) went into his stomach, hit the spine and bounced around, doing considerable damage. Of course, I didn't find out the details until much later. The ambulance got down from Carmel in about fifteen minutes and whisked him away to Community Hospital. One of the attendants told me that if he lived as far as the hospital, he'd probably make it.

After I had done the 911 thing, I had gone back to the wounded man and tried to keep pressure on him to stem the bleeding. The medic told me that my first aid helped to keep him going, but he wasn't sure how long he'd last. They hung a pint of plasma and some saline for him and got away fast.

I had told the sheriff's office all I could on the phone. It was self-defense. Colucci was trying to kill me, so I shot him. I mentioned a few pertinent facts, like that Colucci had started his professional career as a hired gun. They told me to sit tight until a couple of sheriff's units arrived. I told them I didn't plan to go anywhere.

I was hoping for Balestreri to be among the deputies, but when the cop cars got to Greg's place I could see he wasn't one of them. I greeted them at the door.

"Hi, guys. Glad you could come. I'm Pat Riordan. I called. You must have passed the ambulance. It left about five minutes ago. The guy I shot was in it. He was still alive, although they were pretty skeptical about his chances."

Two of the deputies stood about ten feet from the house and tried to decide whether I was crazy or just stupid.

The larger of the two finally spoke: "You called. OK. The way we get it is that this guy was trying to kill you, so you shot him. Right?"

"That's about it. Yeah."

"You claim it was self-defense. Right?"

"That's what I told the dispatcher. Yeah."

The spokesman looked at his partner. Then he turned back to me. "Mr. Riordan, I'm afraid we're going to have to take you in for questioning. *You* say it was self-defense, but neither one of *us* saw what happened. So you'll have to come along with us. If you'll step this way, please."

"Hey, aren't you going to look at the scene of the alleged crime? Don't you want to come in and look at blood stains or something?"

"There's another unit behind us, sir. They're equipped to do that stuff. We're just supposed to pick you up."

The three of us trudged out to the highway. The big black pickup was still blocking Greg's driveway. As we passed my damaged Mercedes, the larger officer looked at me.

"That yours?" he asked.

"Yep."

"How did it get in such bad shape? Looks like a bullet went through that back window."

"You got it."

"Doesn't look like it happened today, though."

"Didn't," was all I would say.

"Oh," said the deputy.

I turned to the other officer, who had a firm grip on my elbow. "You know Tony Balestreri?"

He looked surprised. "Hell, yes. Do *you* know Balestreri?"

"Now, why would I ask you if you knew Tony if I *didn't* know Tony?"

That seemed to confuse the man, so I decided to help him out. "Balestreri is perhaps one of the three or four real friends I have in the world. He knows just what I do, just what I have been involved in recently, and he even knows the guy I shot. Is there any way you can get him on your radio?"

He turned to his partner. "Jerome, is Balestreri on shift today?"

"I think so. He might be at the Monterey Station. Call 'em."

The larger man reached into his car and picked up his radio microphone. In a few minutes he reached Balestreri.

"Riordan?" I could hear Tony's voice roaring over the airwaves. "What has the sonofabitch got into now? Is he there? Let me talk to him."

The officer obediently handed the device to me.

"Hi, Tony, guess what?"

"Don't give me any shit, Pat. What was Bowman talking about? *You* shot somebody? I don't believe it. Guy shot himself, right? You're just faking it for publicity. I've never known you to touch a gun, let alone shoot somebody. At least, since you've been a civilian. And that's been what? Thirty, thirty-five years?"

"Longer, Tony. It was Greg Farrell's gun. Eddie Colucci was chasing me with a very threatening forty-five automatic, so I grabbed one of Greg's guns and shot him. I'm really sorry. I didn't want to have to do it."

Balestreri calmed down a little. "OK. Let those two deputies bring you in to me. Put one of 'em back on."

One of the officers took the microphone from me and exchanged some cryptic law enforcement jargon with Sergeant Balestreri. The guy shrugged and looked at me. Then he got off the horn, pushed me into the hard, cramped back seat of his patrol car, and drove back to Monterey.

Tony was pacing back and forth in front of the Monterey Substation when we got there. I got out of the car, bruised and cramped after the ride from Big Sur. When my feet touched the ground and I tried to stand straight, I thought my knees weren't going to work. I felt like a cowboy who'd been riding the range all day in somebody else's saddle. The joints don't work like they used to, somehow.

"Follow me," said Balestreri, marching into the building. I followed him, like a high school freshman being taken to see the principal.

When we got to his office, he sat on his desk and motioned for me to sit in a convenient chair. He folded his arms and glared for the better part of a minute.

"So. You figured you could duke it out with Eddie Colucci, did you?

Why do you get yourself into such ridiculous situations, Riordan? You got a death wish? So you got shot and it didn't kill you. You got some sort of notion you're immortal?

I spoke calmly, I think. "I didn't know who was following me in that goddam truck. I *did* know that I wanted to lose whoever it was. And the only way I thought I could do it was the way I did it. Dammit, Tony, you know me better than that. You know I don't take crazy chances. You know that I don't use guns. Except this one time. Because, God knows, I needed one."

Some of the stiffness went out of him. He stood up and walked around to his desk chair. "Well, is that it? Now you know who has been gunning for you, so you can breathe easy. From what I hear, Colucci is not going to be out of the hospital for a long time, if he gets out at all. You did a lot of damage with one bullet, man."

"No, it is not *it*. Colucci told me that he wasn't the guy who had been trying to kill me, but that he was going to finish the job. In just those words, as a matter of fact. No, Sergeant, there's still a lot to find out. Who shot me, if Colucci didn't. Who tried to run me down. Where the hell Felicia Montalvo kept her money. Little things like that."

Balestreri drummed his fingers on his desk top. "You want to see your client? You know, the white-haired guy. He's in County Jail over in Salinas, but I could fix it for you. Just mention my name."

"My car is down in Greg Farrell's front yard. I am not going to be able to see anybody right now."

"Your car is being towed in, along with the truck that Colucci used to chase you. It'll be here in a couple of hours. Courtesy of the county."

"What am I supposed to do for a couple of hours? Sit on my ass on one of these hard chairs. I'm crippled as it is from riding in the bad guy seat in one of your patrol cars. Lemme use your phone." I picked it up without waiting for an answer.

"Dial nine for outside," he said, wearily.

I called my office. When Reiko answered I cut her off in the middle of her well-rehearsed official response.

"This is Riordan. Get in your car and come over to the Sheriff's station on Aguajito. And don't ask any questions. Got it?"

She was irritated. "Goddamit, Riordan. . . ." I slammed the receiver down.

She was mad as hell, but she was there for me in ten minutes. She came into Balestreri's office steaming.

"You miserable bastard, who do you think you are to order me around? I . . . am . . . your . . . partner. I am *not* your slave. Got it?"

Balestreri interceded, and I'm damn' glad he did. She was about to pick up a paperweight and use it on me. "Hold it, Reiko. This guy has just shot somebody, maybe fatally. He is in a state of macho, if not shock. He's not responsible for what he does. Slow down."

She had her hand on a large geode that Tony uses as a desk ornament but she stopped, open mouthed. She narrowed her eyes and looked at me in disbelief.

"You . . . shot somebody? Who?"

"Eddie Colucci. Now let's get the hell out of here."

Reiko continued to look at me as if I had suddenly turned into John Wayne. She moved dreamily out the door of Balestreri's office, and walked toward her car, a dazed expression on her face. She didn't bother to ask me what happened. She probably wouldn't have believed me anyhow.

"Where are we going?" she said, after we got in the car. She was being terribly polite now, and making me feel a little guilty for being so abusive with her. Secretly, though, I felt pretty good about the whole thing.

I thought a moment. "Tony thinks we're going over to Salinas to talk to Farnham. Where we are *really* going is to Carmel Point. To Rutledge's, formerly Felicia Montalvo's. Tally ho!"

41

"I'm sorry I can't stay, but I really must be going."

I GUESS I WAS still semi-stunned by the events of the past couple of hours. Reiko's Indianapolis-style driving didn't bother me as she wheeled the Honda out onto Highway One on the way to Carmel Point. She was apparently struck dumb by the knowledge that I had really *shot* somebody. We were speeding south on San Antonio when she finally spoke:

"You shot Colucci. *You*. What with?"

" 'With what?' is better. One of Greg's guns. I guess he keeps it on the night table. Anyhow, there it was. Colucci was trying to put holes in me, so I put one in him. I couldn't see him, but I shot him. Hey, maybe when I was in the Army I should have gone on the pistol range blindfolded. I might have been able to hit the target." It was a weak attempt at humor.

"That was a pretty weak attempt at humor." Reiko gave me a nasty, disapproving look. "Tell me the whole story."

In the ninety seconds that it took us to get to Felicia's house, I told her. She made small Japanese growls under her breath during my tale.

When we pulled up in front of Felicia's—oops, Rutledge's—house, she turned off the ignition and gave me a long look.

"You have been a bleeding pacifist long enough, Riordan. The time has come to do what Tony has been after you to do forever. Apply for a permit. Get a gun. You don't have to use it. *Except* when it becomes *absolutely necessary.* You were lucky this time. You were in Greg's house, and you found one of Greg's guns. Otherwise, that trained assassin would have blasted your brains into the canyon."

I didn't want to admit it, but she was making good sense. Well, I said to myself, I'll think about it. To Reiko, I said: "OK, Mom. I'll do my homework every night and never touch Cynthia Adams on the tits again."

She glared, but I was out of the car and walking towards the house.

When I was halfway up the path, the door opened and through it came a small, gray, bespectacled man I had never seen before, carrying an attache case. He stopped dead when he saw me and hopped on one foot and then the other, as if he were trying to make up his mind to run for cover, or he had to go to the bathroom real bad.

I greeted him expansively. "Hi, there. I'm Pat Riordan, your friendly private eye. And you are. . . .?"

"Giurlani. Fred Giurlani. I'm sorry I can't stay, but I really must be going." For a moment I could hear Groucho singing, "Hello, I must be going." But this guy didn't look anything like Groucho.

"Stay a minute, Fred. I suspect that neither one of us is here without purpose. Is Mrs. Rutledge in?"

"Er, no. She has returned to Glendale, I believe. That is, that's what I've been told." He seemed very nervous.

"May I inquire, Fred, just what you're doing here, if Mrs. Rutledge is not here? Perhaps the fair Lisa Andrews is on the premises, right?"

"There is nobody here, Mr. Riordan. I . . . I . . . found the door open, so I went into the house. I know the Rutledge family only slightly. I was Felicia Montalvo's accountant."

"*Hot damn!*" Reiko shouted into my ear from a distance of about six inches. "He's the guy who knows where the money is. He's here to get the money."

The little man began to tap dance backwards from Reiko, who had leaped ahead of me and was staring him in the face. She was about Giurlani's height, and I'm sure it gave her a sense of power.

"Please. Let's go back into the house, where we can discuss this matter . . . quietly." Giurlani turned and walked back towards the house. Reiko and I followed.

We filed into the familiar hallway, decorated, as every other room in the house, with Felicia Montalvo's counterfeit paintings. In the living room, Giurlani sat down on the couch with his attache case across his knees. I sat in a large easy chair and Reiko perched on one of its arms.

"I must tell you, Mr. Riordan, that I, too, have been aware of Felicia Montalvo's missing fortune. During the years when I handled her financial affairs, her income was very substantial, to say the least. We had a special arrangement. I have an office in Los Angeles. All moneys due Felicia came to me. I had her power of attorney. She instructed me to purchase U.S. Treasury bonds, which I would then mail back to her. Up until 1986, you understand, one could get the actual bond. Nowadays, alas, one must depend on electronics. But, no matter. The income from the bonds would come to me, I would deposit it in an account in Los Angeles, and twice a year I would fly up to Monterey and deliver cash to Felicia. She always managed to get rid of Eric Farnham during my brief visits. So he knew nothing of the agreement between Felicia and me.

"I do not know what the lady did with the bonds. When I arrived here, I had no idea where to look. In the past two hours, I have searched every likely place. The house is in rather a mess, you know. The earthquake dislodged a lot of glassware and dishes. I discovered the remains of what had been a very fine Rookwood vase smashed to bits on the hearth. Pity. But the bonds—nowhere to be found."

"Suppose you found the bonds, Mr. Giurlani. What could you do with 'em?" I think Reiko surprised herself with the question.

"Ah, that is something I really hadn't thought out. With Felicia's power of attorney, I could have, in her lifetime, legally had the bonds transferred into my own name. But that would have been a very dangerous thing to do. I certainly would not be sitting here, talking to you, if I had embezzled from Felicia Montalvo. Now, I suppose, the bonds become the property of Felicia's legal heir. What I had in mind was offering my services to that person for a small percentage."

"How small a percentage?" I spoke up. "Felicia's sister in San Jose is the heir. She's a widow, all alone in the world. What kind of con do you propose to lay on her?"

"*Please*, Mr. Riordan, I do not intend to 'con' anybody. Two or three percent is all I might ask. The bonds are worth millions."

Yeah, I thought, but where the hell are they? I looked around the room. Felicia's paintings covered the walls. Many of them hung askew, the result of the quake of '89. One had fallen from the wall, causing the frame to part at one corner. I walked over and picked it up. It was a copy of Van Gogh's "Sunflowers," as good a counterfeit as I have ever seen. I tried to force the corner of the frame back together, but it was badly sprung. A hopeless task. Then a wild notion struck me.

The canvas seemed unnecessarily thick. I grasped the frame at the break and pulled. A second layer of canvas began to peel off. I yanked on a corner. The two pieces of material came apart. Neatly tucked between the sandwich of canvas was a U.S. Treasury bond with a face amount of one hundred thousand dollars.

42

"You what?" were his first words.

I LOOKED AT Giurlani, he looked at me, and we both looked at
Reiko, who couldn't take her eyes off the beautifully engraved piece of
paper concealed in Felicia's canvas.

"That's where it is," she whispered. "That's where it *all* is. U.S.
Treasury bonds, the safest stash in the world—unless the whole damn'
country goes bankrupt." She turned to Giurlani. "Do you think that
could ever happen? I mean, with the deficit and all? What a shrewd
old bitch she was, Riordan. All that loot in U.S. Treasury bonds. And
I'll bet there's at least one of these lovely pieces of paper in every one
of the old lady's goddam paintings."

She was absolutely right, of course. The long lost treasure of Carmel
Point had been found. But in the minute or so following my discovery
of the bond in the painting, I realized that we couldn't legally touch it.
Or tear open any of the other paintings to see what they contained.

I took a deep breath and put my hand on the skinny shoulder of
Fred Giurlani.

"OK, accountant. Where do we go from here? Does this item
belong to Felicia's heir, or, since the house was purchased as is from
the estate, is it the property of the widow of Harrison Rutledge?"

"I don't know." The little man's glasses had steamed up. The shock of our discovery had raised his blood pressure suddenly. He took off the spectacles and wiped them on his shirt. "This is a legal matter. This bond—and any others that might be found—was the property of Felicia Montalvo. Whether it could be judged the rightful property of the heir or legally the property of the purchaser of the house is. . . ." He stood there with his mouth hanging open.

"Hey, wait." Reiko spoke up. "We're on the premises illegally. If we report this, we're admitting to trespass. Let's take a little time to think through this mess."

So we did. It was finally decided that I should call Balestreri, who, as a personal friend, would hesitate to arrest me, and ask him what to do.

"You *what?*" were his first words. He shouted them into my ear. I held the phone a foot away.

"I told you. We came here. The door was open. That is, the door was unlocked. We knocked. We thought we heard somebody say, 'Come in'. So we came in. That's our story."

He was still very loud. "A picture had fallen off the wall. The frame was busted. You were tryin' to fix it and found a hundred thousand dollar bond?"

"Yeah, Tony." I laughed, unconvincingly. "What do you suppose we ought to do?"

There was silence at the other end. I could hear business as usual in the sheriff's office being carried on in the background. For a moment, I thought Balestreri had fainted or maybe had a heart attack. Just as I was about to say something, he came back:

"Stay there. Stay where you are. I will get hold of a judge. I'm not sure what kind of warrant I need, but I'm thinking of one for your arrest. Anyhow, stay there. Don't move until I get there."

Needless to say, we stayed. We resumed our positions in the room and stared at each other for ten minutes without talking. I don't know what the other two were thinking about, but I was wondering if we *could* be arrested for trespassing.

We were all suddenly brought out of our several dreams by a shrill and raucous voice.

"What the hell are you people doing here? Don't you know this is my mother's house? Get out! Get *out!*"

Lisa Andrews, almost unrecognizable in a tailored suit and a severe white blouse tied at the neck with a black velvet bow, stood in the doorway.

"Hi, Lisa. Long time, no see. Sit down. The sheriff's men will be here any minute." I couldn't think of anything else to say. Lisa told us to get out. Balestreri told us to stay put. I was getting tired, and my sore shoulder was beginning to throb.

She took another tack. "Now, look here. This is my mother's house. She has gone back to Glendale and probably will never return to Carmel." She looked at me with fire in her eyes. "*You,* you bastard. You killed Eddie Colucci, the only man in my mother's life who really cared for her."

So Colucci was dead. I began to feel very depressed. I hadn't even *shot* at anybody for a long, long time, and now I'd killed a man.

"I'm sorry, Lisa. But you know that Colucci was trying to kill me. You know what he was. *You* know what he did to you. How could you have any feelings for him?"

"For *him?* No, no, no. He was an asshole, a creep, a complete sonofabitch. But . . ." Tears glistened in her eyes. She was caught in the grip of an unaccustomed emotion. "She's my mother. In my own way, I love her. Even after she married Rutledge, I loved her. And she loved Eddie Colucci. And you killed him." She sank into a chair and cried like a little girl.

I was on my feet by this time. I knelt in front of Lisa and said, softly: "Honey, I'm sorry. I never wanted to kill anybody. But things happen. Sometimes you can't help what you do. Like your shooting me."

She looked at me, tears still streaming down her face. "How did you know?"

"I guessed. Garcia was right, wasn't he? You were the shooter in the black pickup. You denied it, but it's true. Why did you shoot me?"

"I didn't mean to hit you. I'm a good shot, Riordan. I just meant to put one close to your ear. So you'd get the hell off the case. I figured sooner or later you'd find the old lady's money for Farnham. And I didn't want you to before *we* could." She sniffled. Reiko offered her a tissue.

"What about the hospital? Who put the bullet in the wrong bed at the hospital?"

"That was my snotty brother. Like I told you, he was supposed to really *kill* you, but he chickened out. He's lucky he got out without being caught."

She was truly vulnerable. All the starch had gone out of her. I wondered if covering her navel had taken away her spirit.

"So, who killed your stepfather and, more to the point, who tried to run me down?"

"That was Colucci. He got the keys to the pickup from Jason. He was the professional. He was really pissed that you got away from him in that vacant lot in Carmel. He killed Rutledge the way he'd been trained. Tied him up and put a couple of small caliber slugs in the back of his head."

There was only one more thing I needed to know.

"Lisa, do you know who it was that I saw coming out of an office down on Via Nona Marie? You know, by the post office."

A voice from across the room. "That was me, I'm afraid." Giurlani was polishing his glasses on his shirt tail, pausing occasionally to hold them up to the light. "I was the third party you saw with Colucci and Mrs. Rutledge. We had all three come to Carmel for the same reason. Please believe me, Mr. Riordan, I do not normally associate with people like Colucci. I came to talk with Mrs. Rutledge about, you know, Felicia's fortune. She managed to convince me that I had better cast my lot with her. She and I and Colucci would share the money. Only *I* knew about the bonds. I did not tell them. But I'm afraid I was a witness to the destruction of what was thought to be the only copy of Rutledge's will. I'm sorry for that. Sullies my reputation a bit, doesn't it?"

I was pretty well exhausted after that. All these revelations had drained me. But just as Giurlani finished his contribution to this general confessional, Balestreri arrived with a warrant to enter, a warrent to search, and a warrant to sieze disputed property. I am extremely happy that he didn't have a warrant for my arrest.

43

Reiko appeared in the door, radiant.

A FEW DAYS LATER, in my office, I was trying to explain this whole affair to Sally Morse.

She looked skeptical. "Wait a minute. You say that the little girl in the tight leather outfit showed up dressed like a yuppie business type?"

"Uh, yeah. You see, her mother had taken Lisa under her wing and convinced her that she was much better off living at home, now that mom had control of Rutledge's money."

"But the will was destroyed, wasn't it? That's what the accountant said."

"*That* will was destroyed. What they did not know at the time, but found out a couple of days later, was that Rutledge had made a new will that took precedence over the one they burned in the trash can. It was filed in Las Vegas and was in the possession of the attorney who handled the dead man's interest in the casino. Am I going too fast for you?"

"So what did the new will provide?"

She was relentless, like some big city district attorney closing in on a criminal she had been trying to hang for years.

"It made Mrs. Rutledge the sole heir. See, the first one cut her out, so she wanted him to have expired intestate." Being able to use the law jargon I had learned before I flunked the bar exam years ago gave me a warm sort of feeling.

Sally wasn't satisfied. "But wouldn't the woman be charged as an accomplice in the murder of her husband?"

"She swears up and down that she didn't know that Colucci killed Rutledge. She might be telling the truth. Anyhow, it's for the law to decide."

She shook her head slowly from side to side. "I don't get it," she said. "First that little Lisa floozy swears she didn't shoot you and then she admits she did. Then she tells you the idiot brother shot into the pillow at the hospital. *Then* she says that Colucci was the guy in the black pickup who tried to run you down. And you believe her?"

"It ain't up to me, honey. This thing has to clear the legal hurdles before it's put away. We don't know yet who owns the bonds. And there were bonds in every one of Felicia's paintings. Pretty clever of the old girl. All of her income was funneled through Los Angeles. She had Giurlani scared to death. And she had Farnham badly fooled. That didn't make him a bit happy when I told him about it."

"You told Farnham about it? When did you talk to *him?*"

"Oh, he was in here yesterday. They had to let him out of jail. Lack of evidence. He had picked up some of the information from the guards. They loved him, they did. They were makin' more money doing favors for Farnham than workin' for the Sheriff. So he came here right away."

"Where is he now?"

"Who knows? He walked out of here, muttering vile oaths. I hope I never see the bastard again. But I'm afraid I will."

Reiko appeared in the door, radiant. Her smile cut a swath of charm in the room.

"*Sal*-ly, how are you? It's been so long since you've paid us a visit."

Sally gave me a look that said, "What's got into her?"

Reiko went on: "You know, we're going to have to get together for lunch some day. For some girl talk, and like that. We really ought to become good friends." She skipped around my desk, patting me on the head in transit, and glided out the door.

We heard her in the outer office singing softly. We heard the start-up noises of her computer. In a moment, the printer came on with its bzzt-bzzt, monotonous sound.

I leaned over and whispered to Sally: "I think she's in love."

"What!"

"Shhh, keep it down. I said I think she's in love . . . with Greg Farrell."

"You gotta be kidding."

"No, honey. The girl has succumbed. Had to happen some day."

"I don't believe it."

"So don't. I *think* I was telling you about Farnham, wasn't I?"

"You were making the whole thing up."

"No, please pay attention. Stephanie Rutledge is back in Glendale with her son and daughter, awaiting the decision of the court on the bond thing. Felicia Montalvo's sister in San Jose is also awaiting some sort of judgment. I suspect they'll settle out of court. There's enough money involved for all concerned, even Giurlani, who has struck some kind of arrangement with both of them. Angel Garcia has vanished into East L.A., probably never to be heard from again. At least, in Monterey County. And I am almost completely recovered from my wound. Just a twinge now and then. So why don't we go up to my place and go to bed."

"It's four o'clock in the afternoon."

"So?"

"In the morning, maybe, yes. At night, sure. But *four o'clock in the afternoon?*"

"Lost your sense of adventure?"

Sally stood up and leaned on my desk with one arm. "OK, sport. But I warn you, I've been working out. If you think you can take me, I'll let you try. Wanna wrestle?"

I rose from my chair with dignity, slowly walked around the desk and grasped her elbow.

Reiko was absorbed in her work, and took no note of us as we departed.

And, you know, my wound didn't give me a bit of trouble.

ABOUT THE AUTHOR

Roy Gilligan was born during the first half of the twentieth century on the south bank of the Ohio River near where the great stream admits the Licking. He was nearly famous for a very short while in Cincinnati as a TV-radio personality. In the late fifties and early sixties he wrote a weekly column on advertising for the *San Francisco Chronicle*. Later on he contributed book reviews to that same newspaper and articles to the *San Jose Mercury-News,* the *Monterey Herald,* and *San Francisco Focus* magazine, among many others. For two decades he taught English in a California high school. He lives with his first and only wife in Carmel, California. He has a daughter, Robin, who supervised the cover design of this book, two remarkable grandchildren, and sweet memories of four wonderful dogs: Wendy, Tina, Maggie, and Mandy Lou.

This is the fourth book in the Pat Riordan Mystery series. If you enjoyed it, and want to pursue any of the first three, *Chinese Restaurants Never Serve Breakfast*, *Live Oaks Also Die*, and *Poets Never Kill*, please send $8.95 plus $1.50 postage and handling to:

Brendan Books
P.O. Box 700097
San Jose, California 95170-0097

(California residents add appropriate sales tax.)

These books are available through bookstores that use the R.R. Bowker Company *Books In Print* catalog system, and are distributed to the trade through Capra Press.

Critical comment on *Chinese Restaurants Never Serve Breakfast:*

"The pace of the story and the twists of the plot will hold the interest of the most jaded mystery buff."
—*Southwest Book Review*

"Gilligan's sleuth is likable, his characters (from trendy Carmelites to moneyed Pebble Beachers) ring true, and the author writes with an assured sense of irony between Carmel's charming ambience and troubled residents."

—Howard Lachtman, *The Stockton Record*

More critical comment on *Live Oaks Also Die:*

"This is a book any mystery buff will love, and it will make you want to get a copy of its predecessor, *Chinese Restaurants Never Serve Breakfast.* . . ."
—Jayne Murdock, *Small Press Exchange*

"If you liked that quirky title *Chinese Restaurants Never Serve Breakfast,* you'll love the second outing for Pat Riordan, his assistant Reiko Masuda, and the Monterey Peninsula descriptions."

—*Mystery News*

About *Poets Never Kill:*

". . . a fascinating tale, all wound up in the end in a satisfying manner."
Small Publishers Exchange

There's an epidemic with 27 million victims. And no visible symptoms.

It's an epidemic of people who can't read.

Believe it or not, 27 million Americans are functionally illiterate, about one adult in five.

The solution to this problem is you... when you join the fight against illiteracy. So call the Coalition for Literacy at toll-free **1-800-228-8813** and volunteer.

Volunteer Against Illiteracy. The only degree you need is a degree of caring.

Ad Council Coalition for Literacy